D0408783

CLOTHES MINDED

written by
Chloe Taylor

illustrated by
Nancy Zhang

Simon Spotlight
New York London Toronto Sydney New Delhi

SIMON SPOTLIGHT
An imprint of Simon & Schuster Children's Publishing Division
1230 Avenue of the Americas, New York, New York 10020
First Simon Spotlight hardcover edition February 2015
Copyright © 2015 by Simon and Schuster, Inc.
All rights reserved, including the right of reproduction in whole or in part in any form.
SIMON SPOTLIGHT and colophon are registered trademarks of Simon & Schuster, Inc.
For information about special discounts for bulk purchases, please contact Simon & Schuster Special Sales at 1-866-506-1949 or business@simonandschuster.com.
Text by Caroline Hickey
Designed by Laura Roode
Manufactured in the United States of America 0115 FFG
10 9 8 7 6 5 4 3 2 1
ISBN 978-1-4814-2928-3 (hc)
ISBN 978-1-4814-2927-6 (pbk)
ISBN 978-1-4814-2929-0 (eBook)
Library of Congress Catalog Card Number 2014942152

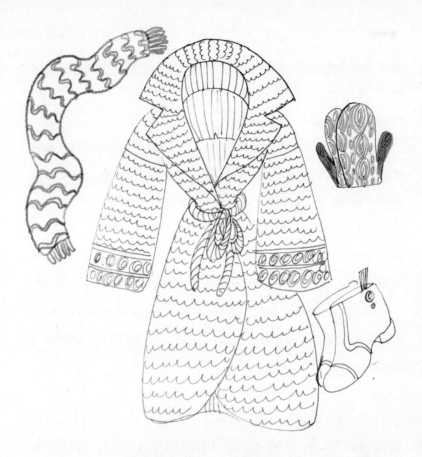

---------- CHAPTER 1 ----------

Nutty for Knitting!

Hello, readers! Your friend Zoey is suffering from a big dose of *reality* at the moment. Everything seems so calm and almost boring after the flurry of planning Aunt Lulu's surprise wedding (in only three weeks). Now that the wedding is over, it's like I'd forgotten what normal life was like with just school, homework, friends, designing and sewing, my blog . . . Oh, yeah—I'm actually still pretty busy!☺

Anyway, I've always wanted to learn to knit, so I just started teaching myself with a book Aunt Lulu gave me, and I've already tried to make a few things, including the scarf in this sketch. My next project might be mittens with different-colored thumbs, but I've heard that gloves and mittens are very difficult! Do any of you knit? If so, please post your helpful tips in the comments! And stay tuned for the (hopefully cozy) results of my knitting projects . . .

Monday mornings were difficult for Zoey Webber. Not because she had a hard time waking up (although she did), and not because she disliked school (she liked it very much), but because her weekends were always so much fun. She spent time with her friends, made pancakes with her father and older brother, and spent hours and hours working on new sketches and designs for her Sew Zoey label.

So even though Zoey was pleased with her Monday morning outfit, which included a skirt made from the top of an old pair of her brother's jeans that she'd stitched to a length of green floral fabric, she found herself sitting in home ec with her chin propped up on her hands, feeling like she was in a bit of a postweekend slump.

One of her best friends, Priti Holbrooke—whose recent penchant for dark, Goth clothes was at odds with her loud, sunny personality—breezed into the room. She complimented Zoey's outfit before plopping down beside her and pulling out her phone to send a text message. Seconds later, Sean Waschikowski, a relatively new friend of Zoey's, plopped down on her other side, even though his assigned seat was across the room.

The bell for class to begin was about to ring.

"Hi, Priti, hi, Sean," Zoey said, her chin still in her hands. She couldn't help wishing she'd been able to sleep in that morning. Even though it was only early fall, the cooler mornings made her want to stay in bed longer.

"You look glum, chum," Sean said.

"I'm not!" Zoey protested. "Honestly. It's just Monday mornings . . . You know. The weekend's over."

Priti nodded sympathetically, slipping her phone into her backpack. "I *do* know," she said. "I've got to switch all my stuff over to my dad's place tonight, because I spent the weekend at my mom's. Ugh."

"I know what you *both* need to cheer up," Sean said, raising his eyebrows and wiggling them. "An inspiring new project!"

Zoey's ears immediately perked up, and with them, her mood. "What do you have in mind?" she asked.

"C'mon, you remember," he said playfully. "I sewed your junior bridesmaid's dress for your aunt's wedding, and you promised you'd owe me one, and then I said we should start a . . ."

"Fashion club!" Zoey finished for him. "That's right; I remember."

Sean drummed his fingers on Zoey's desk. "You got it. My cousin Tessa has one at her high school. Her club is sponsored by their local fashion design college. Most design colleges don't offer sponsorships to middle schools, but I thought we could start the club ourselves here at Mapleton Prep."

"What a cool idea!" Priti responded. "But what is it? A club of fashionable people?"

Zoey shrugged. "I don't know either! Sean, what exactly would the club *do*?"

Sean grinned. "Whatever we want! We'd make it an official club, like the chess club or the musical theater club. And then we'd have to find members, but they don't have to be just designers—fashion clubs are for anyone with an interest in fashion. The people in my cousin's club want to be interior designers, fashion merchandisers, set designers, costumer designers, graphic designers—you name it."

"Then why is it called a fashion club?" Priti asked.

Sean shook his head. "I don't know; I guess that's just how it got started. Or maybe because most of the activities are focused on clothing."

"I don't know anything about starting a club," Zoey said. "I'm not even *in* any clubs at school!"

"But I am—I'm in the musical theater club,"

Sean replied. "And my cousin can fill us in on how her fashion club works to get us started."

"Hmm." Zoey still wasn't sure. She doubted starting a new club was as easy as Sean was making it sound.

"Go on, Zoey," urged Priti. "You know you'll love it if you do it. You'll have more people to talk with about your work! You know I never understand when you try to explain your projects to me."

"That's not true," Zoey said. "And you're learning to sew. You made Buttons's ring-bearer pillow for Aunt Lulu's wedding!"

Priti snorted. "And we all know how *that* turned out," she said, referring to Zoey's new uncle's wedding band falling out of the pillow's pocket and getting lost during the ceremony. Uncle John used Mr. Webber's wedding band for the ceremony, and they didn't find the original wedding band until after the honeymoon.

"But the pillow *looked* great," Zoey said loyally. "And it's not like Buttons understood she wasn't supposed to move around very much! She did her doggie best."

"Do the club," Priti said, refusing to let Zoey change the subject.

"I'll do most of the work, Zoey," Sean pleaded as their home ec teacher, Mrs. Holmes, stood from her desk to begin class. "Please? I just need you for talent and ideas and fashion support!"

Zoey looked back and forth between her old friend and new one, both of whom seemed positive the fashion club and Zoey Webber were destined to be together.

"Oh, all right," Zoey agreed with a grin. "Let's do it, Sean. I do need something new to work on, and my knitting isn't going as well as I'd hoped."

"I can help with that," Sean whispered as he stood up to head to his seat. "My grandmother taught me to knit. But don't tell anyone—it's hard enough for guys at this school to accept that I sew!"

Zoey agreed to meet Sean at school on Tuesday morning to start working on his idea. Sean had made an appointment for them to meet with the principal, Ms. Austen, before homeroom to find out if it was even possible for them to start a new club.

Zoey's brother, Marcus, dropped her off early, so early that the school was eerily silent, and many of the classrooms didn't have their lights on yet. She felt like she had to tiptoe and speak softly in the hallways. She was relieved when she caught up with Sean by his locker and was no longer by herself. Together, they walked to the principal's office.

"You ready?" he asked Zoey. She nodded, not wanting to say out loud that she actually had a few butterflies in her stomach. Even though Zoey had a great relationship with Ms. Austen, who was an admirer of Zoey's designs and blog, Ms. Austen was still the principal, and talking to the principal always felt like a big deal.

Sean knocked boldly on Ms. Austen's door.

"Come in!" Ms. Austen said, opening it and ushering them toward the chairs facing her desk.

Sean and Zoey sat down, and Zoey watched as Ms. Austen opened her travel cup of coffee, stirred in a packet of sugar, and took a careful sip. "Mm," she said. "I've never been a morning person. Coffee helps."

"Now," she continued. "I'm assuming two of my most ambitious students are here early on a

Tuesday morning for a very good reason. How can I help you?"

Sean cleared his throat. "Well, Zoey and I would like to start a fashion club. We want it to be an official club, with a regular meeting day, and field trips and everything, and its focus would be on encouraging students with an interest in all types of design, from clothing to interior to graphic."

Zoey and Sean had talked on the phone the night before, and he'd rehearsed what he was going to say. Zoey thought it sounded great.

Evidently, Ms. Austen did too, because she sat back in her chair, nodding and looking quite pleased. Zoey noticed Ms. Austen was wearing a beautiful vintage Diane von Furstenberg wrap dress and bright blue t-strapped heels that day. If anyone would be sympathetic to their cause, it would be her.

"What a great idea!" Ms. Austen said. "I love to give my students opportunities to explore their passions, especially ones that aren't necessarily addressed in our standard curriculum, although home ec is a start. However, there are a few things we need to consider."

Zoey bit her lip. That sounded serious. "Like what?"

Ms. Austen rocked back and forth in her chair, tenting her fingertips. "The school year is well underway, so the school's budget for clubs has already been divided among the existing clubs."

Sean nodded. "Right, okay."

Zoey hadn't even thought about the club needing a budget. But she supposed that field trips and materials and whatever else they might need would cost money.

"So you'll have to charge dues to your members," Ms. Austen explained. "And you'll need to choose a president for the club, advertise to get members, decide what your dues will be and collect them, choose a meeting day, and so on."

Zoey had her sketchbook with her, as always, and whipped it out to jot down notes.

"And lastly," said Ms. Austen, "you'll need to come up with a plan for meeting activities and find a teacher who will be willing to act as your club's leader and supervisor."

To Zoey, the list was already starting to sound

like a bit more than she'd anticipated. But Sean was leaning forward in his seat, a huge smile on his face.

"That's it? Great!" he said. "So you're fine with us getting started right away?"

Ms. Austen nodded. "Absolutely. I'd be very proud for our middle school to be the first in the area to have a fashion club!"

Zoey and Sean exchanged a look. She couldn't help feeling bolstered by the principal's enthusiasm. It would be neat to do something totally unique at Mapleton Prep. After all, it wasn't the first time Zoey had done something most twelve-year-olds hadn't, including being a judge on the TV show *Fashion Showdown*, making a wedding dress, and having a famous Hollywood starlet wear one of her designs. Starting a club would seem like a piece of cake compared to those things.

A bell rang, signaling that students had three minutes to make it to homeroom. Zoey and Sean gathered up their books to leave.

"Keep me posted," Ms. Austen said. "And thank you for setting such a good example for your fellow students."

Sean and Zoey left the office, moving swiftly in the direction of their homerooms.

"That went great!" Sean said. "This'll be easy."

"Easy?" Zoey repeated. "Ha! We have a lot to do. But I was thinking maybe Mrs. Holmes from home ec might be willing to be our club leader. I can ask her later if you want."

Sean nodded. "I knew I could count on you, Webber!"

Zoey laughed. "We're a good team, Waschi—um . . ."

"Waschi*kowski*. It's a bit of a mouthful, I know," Sean said, shrugging. "But we really are a good team. Fashion club, here we come!"

CHAPTER 2

For a Great *Prints*ipal!

Guess *what?* I've found a new project—but not the kind I usually do. My terrific friend S and I are starting a fashion club at our middle school! It's going to be so cool. We got permission from our school's principal, and our home ec teacher has agreed to be our club leader (and was *sew* nice about it! Thanks, Mrs. H!)

I've never done anything like this before, but S is in the musical theater club, so he knows what he's doing. Plus, he seems to be really good at convincing people to do things he wants. (Ahem . . . like getting me to help him start the club!)

In honor of our school's wonderful, fashionista principal, I've sketched this outfit, which I know would look really great on her. It's got a slight vintage feel, which is her style, but the prints make it modern. Maybe we'll even make it for her as a project in the club!

Zoey sat in her school's auditorium Thursday morning, surrounded by her girlfriends. Ms. Austen had called an all-school assembly, and Zoey and her friends Priti, Kate Mackey, and Libby Flynn, as well as the rest of the student body at Mapleton Prep, were wondering why.

"Maybe they're giving us an extra-long winter break this year?" Priti said hopefully. "Or getting rid of report cards?"

The rest of the girls laughed. Kate, who was

devoted to sports, said, "Maybe she's announcing the soccer team's status in the state championships."

Libby shook her head. "You guys, it's probably just some assembly about a famous scientist or something."

But Zoey didn't think any of those suggestions were right. She could tell by the way Ms. Austen stood at the podium, nervously flipping through papers and tucking her hair behind her ears. The principal had something important to tell them. And Zoey couldn't wait to hear what it was.

"Shh!" Zoey hissed.

Her friends stared back at her, openmouthed.

"Did you just *shush* us?" Priti asked. Kate and Libby giggled, and then Libby very dramatically shushed Zoey back. Zoey couldn't help from cracking a smile.

"Attention, students," Ms. Austen said as a teacher flicked the overhead lights on and off to signal for quiet. She took a deep breath and grinned at the auditorium full of students. "I'm delighted to announce that Mapleton Prep is beginning a *community service program* this year. In fact, it's going to begin right away! Students will be asked to try out several different volunteer opportunities and then select *one* that he or she would like to visit regularly."

The principal paused for a moment, allowing her words to sink in. Zoey caught her friend Kate's eye, and they both nodded. Zoey liked the idea of doing some community service.

"Once you have chosen your service project, you will be asked to complete twenty hours by the end of the school year. This will give you the chance to really invest in something, or some *place*, that will benefit from your time and talents."

"But where will we volunteer?" whispered Libby. "I don't even know where to go."

"To make it easy for you, I've placed sign-up sheets for several volunteer opportunities on the large bulletin board outside the auditorium doors. Some venues will be more popular than others. You are also free to choose other opportunities that are not on the sheets, as long as you have your homeroom teacher sign off on them. Homeroom teachers will be handing out more details about the new community service program later this week. For now, feel free to check out the sign-up sheets and start volunteering! Remember, our community is only as good as the people in it."

The students chatted and clapped, and the principal dismissed everyone. Zoey and her friends jumped up quickly and rushed out the main doors to the bulletin board, anxious to try and sign up for something together before all the lists filled up. They only had a few minutes until class began.

The four girls spread out in front of the board and started reading.

"Look!" said Libby. "The thrift shop needs volunteers this coming Saturday, and there's room for all four of us!"

"Sign us up!" Priti squealed. "Quick!"

Libby whipped out a purple pen and filled in their names. Then she signed herself up for the pet shelter as well, and Zoey, seeing that, added her own name.

"I'd love to play with the animals," Zoey said. "My dad still won't let Marcus and me have a pet, so all I have is my aunt's dog, Buttons. And I don't even see her very much during the school year. The shelter will be great!"

Kate signed herself up to help at the local food pantry, which distributed donated food to families in need, and Priti volunteered to help at the home for the elderly. Satisfied, they moved away from the board to let other kids sign up.

"This new program sounds great," Kate said. "I've been wanting to do some volunteer work, but I didn't know where or how to get started."

"Me too!" Libby exclaimed. "And *I* can't wait to play with the animals at the shelter. I'm already counting down the minutes."

"Ms. Austen is really shaking things up around here," said Priti. "First, she ditched our uniforms, then she added the electives program, and now community service! I wonder what'll be next?"

Zoey grinned. "Why, the fashion club, of course! Stay tuned for more details. I'm meeting with Sean this weekend to figure everything out. It's going to be a whole new world at Mapleton Prep."

"I'm ready for it," Kate said with a laugh. She was wearing her usual uniform of comfortable jeans and a crew-neck sweater. "I've been waiting for something like the fashion club to come along."

"Sean and I are going to make the fashion club so fun, even *you* might join it, Kate Mackey. Even you."

The girls all laughed, then said good-bye as they headed in separate directions for their classes.

Zoey tried to pay attention in her first-period class, but she couldn't stop thinking about how many new things she had going on. First, a new club, and now the service project. It was going to be a busy semester for sure!

Marcus dropped Zoey off at the *What's Old Is New* thrift store on Saturday morning. Inside, she found her three best friends already there, waiting for her to arrive.

"I'm Zoey," she said to the girl behind the counter. The girl was the only other person in the store, so Zoey assumed she was in charge, even though she looked like she was only a senior in high school, about the same age as Priti's sisters. "Sorry if I'm late. What can I do to help?"

"You're not late," said the girl. "I'm Annabel. We just got in a few big bags of donations yesterday. You all could start going through them. You need to decide what's in good enough shape to keep, what needs a cleaning, and what should just be tossed or recycled. Anything that's ripped or stained has to get recycled, okay? Then when you're done, I'll show you where to put everything."

Zoey nodded. It sounded easy enough to her. She followed her friends to the back of the store, where there was an area to sort new donations. The girls got to work.

"This is pretty easy," Libby whispered. "But it's awfully quiet here. I'm not sure they really need four of us volunteering."

"Maybe it gets busy later," Priti suggested. "Who knows?"

"I don't think there were any other options the four of us could do together," Zoey said as she opened a large garbage bag and found a wrinkly ball of women's suits.

"I'm pretty excited to visit the food pantry next week," Kate said. "Although now that I'm back on the swim team, it's going to be hard to work it into my schedule." Kate, who'd had swimmer's shoulder a while back, was finally swimming again after being cleared by her doctor.

"How's your shoulder been since you started swimming again?" Libby asked. "Does it hurt?"

Kate shook her head, smiling broadly. "Nope! It feels as good as new. Taking a few months to rest really was the best thing for it. I've lost a bit of speed, but Coach says it'll come back fast."

Annabel, who was roaming the store, refolding things and dusting as she went, picked up a remote control from somewhere and turned on a TV that hung from the ceiling. She channel surfed until it stopped on an ice-skating competition.

"Wow, guys, look at that!" Zoey said, transfixed.

A young female skater, probably no more than fifteen or sixteen years old, was gliding across the ice to a beautiful piece of music. Her skating appeared effortless, and her jumps were high and confident.

"That's Sonya Turley," said Annabel. "She's probably going to win the national championships in a few weeks. She's a big deal."

The music was perfect for her skating—classical, but slightly jazzy at the same time. "What's this song?" Zoey asked.

"I think it's Gershwin's *Rhapsody in Blue*," said Annabel.

Zoey watched as the blue fabric of Sonya's costume moved like liquid and seemed to match the rhythm of the music perfectly. How amazing to be able to skate like that, to move to that beautiful music!

Inspired, Zoey grabbed her bag and pulled out her sketchbook. Kate, Priti, and Libby continued to sort and fold clothes, exchanging a knowing look over Zoey's head. They knew their friend, and when she was inspired, she *had* to sketch.

"I can't believe I've never made an ice-skating outfit before," Zoey muttered as she worked on her sketch. "They're so beautiful. And the way they move and change with all the wind from the skater's speed. It's amazing!"

"That skirt looks awesome, Zoey," Priti commented, leaning a bit over Zoey's shoulder so she could see it. "It almost looks like those overhead fringe-y things at a car wash."

Zoey laughed. "That's kind of what I was think-ing. It's a car-wash skirt with piano-key detailing on it! Wouldn't it look amazing on the ice?" Zoey put a few finishing touches on her sketch and then tucked it safely back into her bag.

Even though her mind was still picturing Sonya Turley whirling around the ice, she had work to do at the thrift shop, and that came first.

------- CHAPTER 3 -------

Rhapsody in Blue *Fabric*!

Well, readers, things have reeeeeally gotten interesting at school lately. Not only did they add an electives program (my home ec class!), we now have a community service program that allows us to get out and help people! I volunteered at the neighborhood thrift shop this morning, but instead of being inspired by all the beautiful vintage clothes, I ended up obsessing over beautiful figure skater Sonya Turley, who was performing in a competition on TV! Have you seen her? She's ah-*ma*-zing, and she was wearing the most elegant, perfectly made costume. All the skaters do, actually. I think I was *almost* more impressed by their costumes than by all the camel spins and triple loop jumps!

Anyway, after watching Sonya skate her long program (do I sound like I know what I'm talking about? Cuz I don't! Hee-hee), I sketched this outfit, which I think would be perfect for her. There's not much point in me sewing it, however, because where would I ever wear it? I can barely do a snowplow stop! Ah well. At least I can enjoy looking at the sketch. . . .

Zoey arrived at Tea Time at exactly two o'clock Sunday afternoon. She craned her neck to see over all the customers sitting at small tables, enjoying tea and cupcakes on a beautiful weekend. Finally, she noticed a long arm waving to her from the back, and Zoey made her way to the table Sean had found for them.

"Hi, hi!" Zoey sang. "I'm so glad you suggested this place. I love their carrot cake cupcakes—yum."

Sean nodded. "Me too. They just started selling these awesome new hybrid pastries, so I ordered one already."

"What's a hybrid pastry?" Zoey asked, baffled.

"It's like a mash-up of a croissant and a doughnut. My parents took me to New York a few weeks ago to see a show, and we had them somewhere, and now they're starting to make them at a lot of different bakeries."

"I'll try one!" Zoey said. Sean flagged down their waitress and ordered a croissant-doughnut for Zoey, and Zoey asked for some tea as well.

"I love your cuff links," Zoey said, grabbing Sean's wrist. He was wearing a lavender button-down with a plaid sweater-vest, and the French cuffs of his shirt sported cuff links shaped like tiny black mustaches. "They're adorable!"

Sean smiled. "Thanks. From my mom."

"She has good taste," Zoey declared. Not for the first time, Zoey looked Sean over and was impressed by his outfit. It was so refreshing to have a guy friend who knew a lot about fashion and clothes and was also really fun to be with. She could really *talk* with him about all the projects she was working on. Suddenly, she wondered if that was how her long-time best friend, Kate, felt sometimes when she hung out with her soccer friends, as opposed to with Zoey. Even though their friendship was special in a different way, Zoey never really understood most of the sports stuff Kate was talking about.

The tea and pastries arrived, and after a few hurried bites, Sean whipped out a notebook. "So, let's talk business. Here's what I'm thinking: we need to figure out a name for the club, who can be in it, and what we'll do. *Go.*"

Zoey choked on a laugh, her mouth full of delicious warm flakes of pastry. "Well, as for who can be in it, I say everyone. I don't like clubs that are exclusive. They just make people feel bad. So even if someone knows *nothing* about fashion or sewing, but they want to join, I think we should say yes."

Sean nodded his head quickly and wrote down "Everyone!" "I agree. I don't think it's the kind of club someone who wasn't genuinely interested would join anyway. So how about a name for it? I was thinking the Sew Zoey Fashion Club."

Zoey nearly gagged. "*No*, no way. I don't want the club to be named after me! That sounds so . . . braggy. No, let's just make the club its own thing, with a name that's fun and fashion-y."

Sean rolled his eyes. "You're too modest, Zoey. Your name is a big draw! You're the most famous person in our middle school."

Zoey laughed. "I'm not sure that's true, but let's keep my name out of it, please. I want this club to be fun, and not related to the stress of my blog and business and stuff. Okay?"

Sean pretended to pout. "*Okay*," he agreed.

Zoey thought for a moment. "How about Threads? That's cute."

Sean chewed his lip. "Cute, but maybe too cutesy. Ditto for Buttons or Zippers."

Zoey laughed out loud again. "The Zippers! That's awesome. Sounds like a punk band or something."

"No guys will join if it's called Threads or Zippers," Sean promised.

"How about the Fashion Fun Club?" Zoey suggested. "That says exactly what it is, so people who join it will know. Just like the musical theater club and the Spanish club."

"Hmm," Sean said. "Fashion Fun Club. It's pretty good. It's a little cheesy, but I kind of like a little cheesy."

"Me too," said Zoey. "Great! We have a name, and everyone can join. Check and check. Now we just need some people to *want* to join. . . ."

Sean polished off the last of his tea and pastry. "Well, I could make some flyers later today and print them up. Then we could meet at school early tomorrow morning and hang them around. What do you think?"

"Sure!" Zoey said. She already liked having Sean as a partner. He had good ideas and had no problem volunteering to do work. Plus, he knew about a lot of great things, like croissant-doughnut hybrids.

He wrote down more notes on his pad. "I'll put the name of the club and that the first meeting is Wednesday in the home ec room after school."

"Why Wednesday?" asked Zoey.

"Because that's when Mrs. Holmes said she could do it, remember?" he said.

"Oh, yeah." Zoey shook her head. "I totally forgot! And I'm the one who asked her. Okay, so you'll make the flyers, and I'll help hang them tomorrow. You're not going to put our names on the flyers or anything, right?" she asked. "I don't want it to be about me."

Sean shook his head. "No, Miss Modesty. I won't mention that the famous Sew Zoey will be in the club. Deal?"

Zoey nodded. "Deal. Let's get out of here. I've been working on this sketch for an ice-skating costume, and even though I'll probably never make it, I've been playing with a muslin sample, just to see how hard it would be to construct."

"Sounds pretty neat. Maybe we can talk about it at the *club* on Wednesday."

"Yay!" Zoey exclaimed as they paid their check and prepared to leave. "By the way, what are we going to *do* at the first meeting?"

"I've already figured that out," Sean assured her. "I'll be in charge of this week's activity, and you can be in charge of next week's. All I need is for you to bring a stack of old fashion magazines, if you have any."

"*If* I have any? Ha!" Zoey chuckled as they pushed the door and walked out to the sidewalk. "Oh, Sean, you have no idea."

Zoey and Sean met early at school the next morning. True to his word, Sean had a stack of flyers with him, printed on differently colored sheets of paper that were sure to stand out and attract attention. They decided to each take half the stack and divide and conquer, since their school was relatively big.

Zoey headed down the math and science wing, toward the gymnasium, with her stack. As she stopped to post one on the bulletin board by the gym, her friend Gabe Monaco came in one of the side doors.

"Hi, Gabe!" she said. "You're here early."

He nodded. "Yeah, I left some photos I developed to dry in the photo lab yesterday, and I wanted to see how they turned out. What are you doing?"

She held up one of the sheets of paper. "Recruiting for the Fashion Fun Club I'm starting with Sean. It's going to be great—it's for people interested in all kinds of design, not just clothing."

"Really? Like what?" Gabe asked. He took a flyer from her and skimmed it.

Zoey explained about Sean's cousin's fashion club and how it included graphic designers, interior designers, and the like. She knew Gabe wanted to be a photographer, but she wasn't sure how he'd view the club.

"You know," he said, "I might come to your meeting. I'd like to do some fashion photography one day, so it wouldn't hurt to learn a little bit about the fashion business. I really don't know anything, other than what I read on your blog! Can I come?"

Zoey was flattered and very pleased. "Of *course!* We'd love to have you there. Wow, thanks, Gabe."

Zoey's insides suddenly felt warmer at the thought of Gabe coming to the club. He had always been a good friend to her, but recently she couldn't help feeling a little more than just friendly toward him. Unfortunately, he'd begun hanging out with their school's visiting French student, Josie, and they looked pretty couple-y to Zoey.

"I'll be there," Gabe promised. "And I might bring Josie, too, if that's all right. You know how much she loves fashion."

Zoey nodded, careful to keep her smile on her face. She liked Josie, and Josie's fashion sense, but Zoey couldn't help feeling *slightly* disappointed that Gabe wouldn't be coming by himself. Oh well. She supposed that would be too good to be true.

"I've got to hang the rest of these flyers, Gabe. I'll see you later!"

Gabe waved and walked off toward the photo lab while Zoey finished her work. Then she met back up with Sean by the home ec classroom. Kids were arriving now, and Sean reported that he'd had a few kids ask him questions about the flyers already. A girl named Sarah from their home ec class, who was very quiet and an excellent handsewer, had told him she'd been waiting for the school to start a fashion club, and she volunteered to help set up before the meeting.

"Wow!" said Zoey. "That's great. So people might really show up!"

Sean shook his head at her and laughed. "Zoey,

it's going to be great. Have a little faith!"

She smiled. "I do. I have faith that you know a lot about fashion clubs *and* that you've done a great job getting this one started. Therefore, I nominate you to be president!"

Sean blushed but looked pleased, as if maybe he'd been hoping all along that things would turn out that way but hadn't wanted to say anything. "Well, okay," he agreed. "I'll be president if you'll be the vice president and treasurer."

Zoey nodded quickly, and they shook hands. "Deal. Here's to the Fashion Fun Club!"

As the two filed into the home ec room before the bell rang, Zoey couldn't help thinking how pleased she was to have a new project to focus on, since all the work and excitement from her aunt's surprise wedding was over. She hadn't realized how much she'd missed having something to plan.

CHAPTER 4

Treasurer and VP! Who, *Me*?

What would a newly elected vice president and treasurer of a fashion club wear? Why, this awesome dress, of course, paired with a "coin purse"! I love playing with traditional symbols like a dollar sign and making it look like something geometric and playful.

And I love that men's-style shoes have come back in! I really want to get a pair of oxfords or loafers to wear with tights.

As you may be guessing from the title and sketch on this post, things with the fashion club S and I are starting are going really well so far, and I'm looking forward to our first meeting on Wednesday! S is in charge of this week's activity, and my aunt has generously donated a stack of old fashion magazines for us to use. I couldn't bring my own magazines, because S informed me that we'll be cutting them up, and I couldn't bear to do that to mine! It'd be sacrilege, in my opinion.☺ But luckily my aunt came through for me with a pile, including some copies of my favorite, *Très Chic*!

Oh, and woof! Meow! Tweet! Those are the sounds of the new friends I'll be making when I volunteer at the pet shelter after school today for the first time. *I can't wait!*

Zoey and Libby waited out in front of the school after the dismissal bell. Marcus would be picking them up any minute to take them to the animal shelter.

Zoey had worn what she thought would be an appropriate outfit to help out with the animals—black-and-white zebra-print leggings and a long pink sweater with the face of a tiger knitted on it. Animal faces and prints were great for mixing and matching, and she'd felt feisty all day at school in it, despite the dreary rain. The rain had finally stopped and the sun had come out, and now Zoey could hardly contain her excitement to see all the animals.

"I just want to hold some kittens," Libby said anxiously. "I looooove kittens."

"Me too," said Zoey. "And puppies. This shelter is where my aunt Lulu adopted Buttons, and when we went to pick her out, they let us hold a bunch of the pups! It was great."

Marcus pulled up, and Zoey wasn't at all surprised to see his girlfriend, and Zoey's good friend, Allie Lovallo in the front seat. Marcus and Allie were together more often than not.

"Hi, Allie," said Zoey. "What's up?"

Libby and Zoey both climbed into the backseat, and Allie turned around to look at them. "It's so neat you're going to volunteer at the animal shelter! They didn't have a community service program when I was at Mapleton Prep."

Zoey nodded. "Yeah, everybody's excited about it. A bunch of kids are doing a park cleanup this weekend!"

Allie shook her head in disbelief. "Our high school doesn't even have a program like that. Maybe I should tell the principal about it."

The shelter wasn't far away, and when they pulled up, Marcus glanced in the rearview mirror and said, "Now, Zoey, you know how Dad feels about pets. Don't come home with fourteen different puppies and kittens you've decided to adopt. Okay?"

Marcus sounded stern, but Zoey knew he secretly would love a dog too. But with both he and Zoey gone all day at school, and Mr. Webber at work as a sports therapist on Eastern State University's campus all day, there would be no one home with the dog. And Mr. Webber thought pets should have some company.

"I won't," Zoey promised. "Or at least I'll *try* not to."

They walked toward the shelter, and Allie eyed the animals in the window wistfully. "Marcus, let's go in for a second—just to see the puppies."

Marcus looked as if he were about to say no, but then when he saw the earnest expression on Allie's face, he changed his mind. "Okay," he agreed. "Just for a few minutes."

As the four of them climbed out of the car, Zoey noticed Allie's outfit: a beautiful silk print blouse and a pair of riding pants.

"Great blouse!" Zoey said. "Did you make that?"

Allie smiled and shook her head. "No, I just bought it. This is the first time I've worn it."

They all walked into the shelter and were pleased to see it was a clean, happy place. Zoey had remembered it being that way, but she knew that some shelters could be rather depressing, with so many animals waiting for adoption.

"Welcome!" said a man with a yellow smiley face T-shirt. "I'm Stephen, the manager here. And which of you are Libby and Zoey, my volunteers for this afternoon?"

The girls raised their hands and introduced

themselves. Then Allie spoke up. "Stephen, my boy-friend and I aren't part of the volunteer program, but we'd love to help out a little bit today if you need us. We could play with some lonely puppies or something?"

Stephen looked them over and sort of shrugged. "Well, we're not supposed to have more than two volunteers at one time, because of our space con-straints. But we've got a few big dogs who aren't getting enough exercise in the doggie yard, and they could use a nice walk outside now that the sun is out. Why don't you two take those four dogs—two each—for a fifteen-minute walk or so? It would really make their day."

Allie's face broke into a smile, and she and Marcus quickly agreed. Stephen helped them clip leashes onto the excited dogs' collars, and let them out the back door. Then he turned to Zoey and Libby, who were looking longingly at all the cages in the room behind them.

"Now, for my *official* volunteers," Stephen said with a wink. "I'd love it if you girls could help me clean out some of these cages, make sure all the animals get fresh water, and then record that on these charts on the wall here. When all that is done, it's playtime! You can take turns pulling out these kitties and pups and playing with them on the floor for a few minutes, and then return them to their cages."

Libby looked positively thrilled. Zoey felt pretty thrilled herself. This was so different from her usual after-school activities of sewing and homework! And all the animals looked so happy to see them. The girls quickly got to work.

Cleaning out the cages was simple, since the dogs were potty trained. The pups just needed their cages wiped down, the ragged towels they used to snuggle with replaced, and their water bowls rinsed and refilled. With both girls working together, it didn't take long to make progress. They were soon sitting on the floor with puppies and kittens crawling on them. Zoey felt like she was in heaven. One pup in particular, who looked like a terrier mix of some sort, seemed to like Zoey a lot and kept rubbing her doggie nose against Zoey's cheek.

"I forgot to tell you!" Libby said as she rubbed

the bellies of two kittens who purred loudly in her lap. "I was sitting next to Gabe in computer science today, and he said he's planning to come to your fashion club meeting tomorrow."

"He told me he might," Zoey said. A second later she added, "He said he's bringing Josie, too."

Zoey had never mentioned to any of her friends that she might like Gabe. She didn't feel comfortable saying something like that about a boy who was already going out with another girl. And, anyway, she and Gabe had been friends for so long, she wasn't completely sure that *was* how she felt. Maybe boy-girl friendships were different from girl-girl ones. Although, she was friends with Sean and didn't feel about him the way she did about Gabe.

"I didn't know Josie was interested in fashion," said Libby. "Although she always looks great."

Zoey scratched the friendly terrier behind the ears and didn't reply.

"I wish I could join the club too!" Libby sighed, replacing the two kittens she'd been playing with and taking two more from a different cage. "But I've got ballet rehearsals every week, and now volunteering, plus homework, so my mom won't let me add another activity. She says I have to 'decide what's most important.'"

"I get it," said Zoey. "Don't worry! I'll fill you in on everything after the meetings."

Libby was about to reply when the back door of the shelter opened and four large dogs burst in, followed by Marcus and Allie, who were both soaking wet.

"What happened?" Zoey asked, jumping up to look around for something to help them dry off. "You look like you fell in a river."

Allie grimaced and looked down at her outfit. "The black lab just *loves* puddles. He ran into every single one and then kept shaking himself off next to me! You wouldn't believe how strong he is!"

Marcus shook his head. "He's a *dog*, Allie. That's what dogs do!"

Allie glared at Marcus. "This is a brand-new blouse that I just bought with money from my Etsy site! I didn't think walking a few dogs would be like being pulled through a *swamp*."

"Calm down, you're overreacting."

Zoey had never heard Marcus and Allie being so snippy with each other. They usually got along well, and if anything, were too lovey-dovey together.

Stephen heard the commotion and came into the back room. "Yikes, guys! You really got soaked. Let me see if I can find you some towels. . . . We're always running out of them, unfortunately, because we use so many for the crates, and for young pups to cuddle up with in place of their mothers. Anyway, they get worn out quickly."

He hunted around in a closet and managed to find them each a small towel. Marcus patted at himself a bit, then gave up and handed his towel to Allie, who was still pretty upset about her blouse.

Zoey and Libby exchanged glances, both aware of the chill between the normally happy couple. But they didn't have time to dwell on it, because Stephen said, "You all have done such a great job today, I have a treat for you!"

He disappeared into another room, and came back with a teeny-tiny pinkish kitten. "She's brand-new!" he said. "Born yesterday. Would you each like to hold her?"

"YES!" Zoey, Allie, and Libby said at the same time. Marcus laughed, and the tension from earlier seemed to dissipate. The four of them took turns cradling the precious tiny kitten, and Zoey couldn't remember having more fun.

"I love cats," Allie declared. "Look how sweet this little kitten is, Marcus!"

Marcus held the kitten for a moment, then handed it to his sister. "Cats are okay, but I prefer dogs. Especially big, wet, puddle-loving dogs. Except when they ruin your clothes, of course."

"Ha-ha," said Allie, still gazing at the tiny kitten.

Libby said, "That's funny—I thought cat people and dog people usually didn't go together!"

Allie and Marcus looked at each other, and Marcus smiled. Then Allie did too. Their silly fight, whatever it was, was over.

"I still like dogs," Allie said. "But I want a cat for sure. I'm going to call my parents when we leave and ask if we can adopt one!"

Zoey gasped. "You are? Oh, that's so great. I'd love to see one of these kitties go home with someone. Do you think they'll say yes?"

Allie shrugged. "I'm not sure. It'll take some convincing, probably, but I think I can get them to come around."

Marcus groaned. "Allie, do I have to give you the same warning I gave Zoey? You can't come home with a new furry friend or three every time you visit the shelter! Your parents will hate me!"

Everyone laughed. Zoey looked wistfully at the kitten as Libby helped Stephen put it back in a private nook with its mother and brothers and sisters. A Webber family pet would be so nice. But for now, taking care of lots of animals at the shelter was *almost* as good!

-------- CHAPTER 5 --------

Cat Woman!

Guess what? *I love animals!* I always knew I liked animals, and I love my "cousin" Buttons, but after my first volunteer day at the pet shelter, I can now say that I am officially passionate about all things small and furry. ☺ I loved all the kittens and the puppies and the older dogs, even the two parrots that were there! In honor of the newborn kitty I got to hold, I made this sketch of an outfit a cat lover might wear . . . and *obviously* the fur is faux!

Last night my brother's girlfriend said that her parents had agreed to let her adopt both an older cat and a kitten! I'm *sew* jealous. But at least I'll be able to visit them at her house. She's planning to go pick them out this coming weekend. Maybe she'll let me help name them!

Also—ahem, ahem—big day today, fashion readers: It's the first meeting of the Fashion Fun Club! If you've ever heard of a fashion club, or been a part of one, leave me a note in the comments. I'd love to hear your ideas on some activities we could do during meetings!

Zoey wondered all day what the first Fashion Fun Club meeting would be like. Every time she saw Sean in the halls, she looked at him nervously, and he grinned and shook his head at her. As a cofounder, she felt like she was responsible for the club being a success, and what if no one showed up? What if it turned out to be a big joke, and she and Sean just sat in the home ec room all by themselves? She could hardly concentrate in her classes, she was so preoccupied.

At last the final bell rang, announcing the end of what had been a very long day for Zoey. She stopped by her locker to grab the stack of magazines Lulu had donated and to quickly check her phone for messages. While scrolling her in-box, she came across the name Sonya Turley and had to lean against the lockers to steady herself. Could it be the *real* Sonya Turley e-mailing her?

She clicked on the message to open it.

Dear Sew Zoey,

I hope you don't mind me e-mailing you! A friend sent me a link to your blog with the ice-skating costume you designed for me. I'm so flattered! And I *love* the design with the car wash skirt and piano-key detailing so, so much. Would you be willing to let my costumer make this outfit for me? She knows my measurements and makes all of my costumes by hand so they fit me perfectly. We'd be more than happy to pay for your design and give you full credit, of course!

I'd like to wear it to the nationals competition in a few weeks so please let me know as soon as you can!

Your friend,

Sonya Turley

PS I love your blog! I can't stop reading it and wondering what you'll design next!

Alone in the hallway, Zoey gasped. *Sonya Turley*, one of ice-skating's most exciting young skaters, wanted to wear a costume Zoey designed to the national championships! Zoey couldn't believe it. She just couldn't! She'd sketched that outfit thinking it would never ever get made, not even for fun. And if Sonya had it made and ended up wearing it, it would be on *national television*.

Zoey felt like she'd won the fashion lottery. Her phone beeped, signaling the start of the Fashion Fun Club meeting, and with a jolt she realized that meant she was already late! The home ec room was on the opposite end of the school. Hurriedly, she grabbed the stack of magazines and attempted to shut her locker with her foot. But the magazines were so heavy, she started to lose her balance, and the whole slippery stack flew out of her arms and onto the floor.

"Argh," Zoey growled. She shut her locker properly, then stooped to collect the magazines and pile them more carefully into her arms. Slowly, she proceeded down the hall. By the time she reached the home ec room, the muscles in her forearms were aching, and she'd practically forgotten the Sonya Turley news. She just knew she was late and that wasn't very "VP and treasurer" of her.

Sean had grouped a few tables together so that the club could sit in a circle, and was distributing scissors and glue sticks to each seat. There were a few kids already at the meeting, including Gabe and Josie, and one or two people Zoey recognized as being in musical theater club and friends of Sean's. There was a girl named Emily from home ec, who bragged a lot about her mother—the chef at a local restaurant—but seemed to have a knack for sewing. So far, a decent turnout.

"Sorry," Zoey puffed as she gently eased her burden down onto the table.

"Wow," said Sean, eyeing the giant stack of high-end fashion magazines, some of which were Italian and French. "Great job, Zoey! Those will be perfect."

"No problem!"

She looked around to see if there was anything she could do to help Sean, but he had just sat down at the head of the table and seemed ready to begin. She took a seat about halfway around the table herself and noticed he'd also handed out large squares of card stock already.

"I'm ready for my close-up, Sean," someone boomed as they walked into the room. "This is going to be ahhhh-maaaaazing."

Without even turning her head, Zoey knew the owner of that voice. It was Ivy Walker, her long-time adversary who had consistently insulted Zoey's outfits for most of the school year.

Zoey turned to look at Ivy, and as their eyes met, Ivy's face went from giddy to sour. Zoey's nearly did the same, but she managed to clench her jaw and keep her expression as neutral as possible. She was

the VP and Treasurer; she couldn't frown at someone who had shown up to join the club.

"Hold up," said Ivy. "No one said Zoey Webber
was going to be part of the Fashion Fun Club. That
would make it the *Un*fashionable *Un*fun Club."

Sean rolled his eyes at Ivy, and said calmly,
"Honestly, I don't understand girls. Ivy, you *know*
you admire Zoey's talent, so chill out. This club is
for *fun*. It says so in the name."

He smiled at the group, as if the whole conversation was in jest, and Ivy wasn't being deadly serious.

Ivy, who seemed stunned to have someone talk
to her like that, abruptly sat down next to Sarah,
the girl from Zoey's home ec class. Either Ivy really
wanted to stay, Zoey thought, or she couldn't help
respecting Sean for standing up to her and wanted
to hear what he had to say.

Zoey reminded herself to be open-minded about
Ivy's presence in the Club. After all, she herself had
decided that anyone could join! She tried to ignore
the tiny voice inside her that kept whispering, *But I
didn't know "anyone" would include Ivy. . . .*

"Great," said Sean, clapping his hands together.

"Let's begin! Welcome to the Fashion Fun Club! Zoey and I will be leading the club together, but we want this to be collaborative, so please be vocal with your suggestions. Mrs. Holmes is our supervisor," he paused, nodding his head in the direction of Mrs. Holmes's desk in the corner, where she sat working on her computer. She waved to the group. "But we'll be running the show ourselves."

"That's right," Mrs. Holmes said. "This is a student-run club, and I expect you all to listen to Sean and Zoey, who are giving their time and energy to create this club for our school. I'm here for backup support as needed."

Zoey hadn't even noticed the teacher when she came in, but she wasn't surprised to hear that Mrs. Holmes was going to take a backseat during club meetings. Mrs. Holmes liked students to take charge. Even so, Zoey couldn't help thinking part of Mrs. Holmes speech had been directed at Ivy for her snarky comment earlier.

Sean pointed to Zoey then, indicating it was her turn to talk.

"Um, right, okay." Zoey stumbled over her words,

having been lost in thought about Mrs. Holmes and Ivy. "Um, I'm VP and treasurer, and since this club is getting started late in the year, we'll need to collect dues, so we can have a budget to be able to afford materials, field trips, or other things. You probably saw that on the flyers. We'll also try to get some things donated, of course, but for now, everyone needs to please hand in your thirty dollar dues to me."

Zoey watched as only three of the people there passed money her way. Ivy was one of them, which was a huge surprise to Zoey, as it most likely meant that Ivy was genuinely interested in the club, and intended to come back for future meetings.

Zoey tucked the money into an envelope she'd marked "Dues." "Okay, so everyone who didn't remember today, please try and bring it next time, so we can start planning the fun stuff."

She nodded at Sean, and he took over again. "So, you're all probably wondering, what are we going to do today? Well, I thought it might be neat to make lookbooks, sort of like you'd find online. Everyone will be given a picture of this one item—today it's a cobalt-blue skater skirt—and then scavenge through these magazines to assemble a complete *look* for this piece. When you have all your pieces, glue them onto the card stock, and we'll compare looks at the end!"

Zoey saw a few smiles around the table, and she couldn't help feeling excited by the activity herself, despite the fact that they'd be cutting up issues of some of the most fantastic fashion magazines. She knew she could do a lot of neat things with that simple skirt and she'd never made a lookbook with magazine clippings before.

"Can we make it a competition?" Ivy asked. "You know, vote on the best one at the end?"

Zoey resisted the urge to sigh. Of course Ivy would have to take something that was purely intended for fun and make it about winning. But Zoey kept quiet, and Sean shrugged and said, "Sure, why not?"

Zoey got to work and was quickly absorbed in finding the right pieces for her lookbook. A few minutes went by, and she noticed Gabe walking around taking pictures.

"Hey, Gabe, thanks for coming," she whispered, not wanting to disturb everyone else.

His cheeks flushed. "Uh, I hope you don't mind, Zoey, but I have *no idea* how to put together a, um, lookbook, so I thought I might take a few shots of your club to use in the yearbook. I joined that committee, too."

Zoey brightened. "Yeah, of course! Great idea." She glanced over at Josie, who was working intently on her project, and Zoey could already see a she'd paired the skirt with a long red trench coat and leopard-print boots. Fierce. Zoey loved it.

When everyone had finished and presented their lookbooks to the group, Sean suggested they vote by silent ballot, and as everyone passed up small scraps of paper to the front, she began to feel nervous. She wasn't sure if she should *want* to win, because she was the most experienced person there, or if she shouldn't want to win, because she was one of the leaders, and therefore it would be like a teacher getting the best grade on a test. She settled for silently hoping Ivy wouldn't win, and feeling kind of bad about it.

After Sean did a quick private ballot count under the table, Zoey was pleased when he announced that Josie had won. Anyone was better than Ivy, plus Josie's lookbook had genuinely been awesome.

"So we'll be meeting here every Wednesday, guys," Sean said at the end of the meeting, "and doing different activities each week. If you have suggestions, come find me or Zoey to discuss. We're open to anything!"

Ivy raised her hand. Zoey looked at Sean questioningly, as if to say, *Why is she raising her hand?*

But Sean just said nicely, "Yes, Ivy?"

Ivy turned to look pointedly at Zoey. "I was wondering if Sew Zoey could use some of her connections to book us a field trip to a fashion show or to meet an editor of a magazine or something. After all, she's *so famous*, right?"

Zoey felt her cheeks grow hot. Ivy was really living up to her namesake: She was being poisonous. Zoey wished Ivy had never heard about the fashion club. In the corner, Mrs. Holmes turned her head from her computer and looked at Zoey. Zoey thought she saw Mrs. Holmes give her a wink, but she wasn't sure. In any case, it gave Zoey a second to collect herself before answering.

"I'd like to do all of that, Ivy," Zoey said evenly. "But I'm afraid I don't have enough connections yet to get the whole club into a show. I haven't even been to a real fashion show yet myself! But I'll keep it in mind." She paused, thinking about her huge news about Sonya Turley, and wanted to announce it just to shut Ivy up. But she knew that wasn't the right thing to do. In fact, it might make Ivy even meaner toward her. Instead, Zoey added, "I *am* going to try and work some local connections, like fabric stores, to get us some donated material, and I'd like to ask you all to please save magazines for future projects. I usually save my own copies for future inspiration, so it's really hard on me to cut them up! These were from my aunt. And check your own homes for extra fabric, buttons, notions, and the like."

"Great point, Zoey," Sean said. "And everyone— bring your dues! Don't make Zoey nag you. She's a busy girl, running her *business* and all."

Even though Sean didn't look at Ivy when he

said the last part, Zoey knew it was intended for her, and she was thankful he was on her side.

And so the meeting ended on an upbeat note, though somewhere deep in the pit of her stomach, Zoey worried Ivy would end up ruining the club. Maybe not for everyone, but for Zoey, at least.

------- CHAPTER 6 -------

All About the Legs!

It's all about the legs . . . in this outfit (chevron tights!), and in the competitive sport of ice-skating. Right? And do you know why I *can't stop* thinking about ice-skating? Because the amazing Sonya Turley has decided to buy the piano-inspired skating costume I designed! NO,

REALLY!!! I can't believe they're paying me for it, but Sonya insisted. Her personal costumer (doesn't that sound awesome? To have a personal costumer?) is going to make the outfit, and Sonya's planning to wear it to nationals in a few weeks. I can hardly believe it. Sonya and I are making a few tweaks to the design now over e-mail, because she's in California at her training facility working hard to get ready to compete. (I love typing things like "getting ready to compete . . .")

Anyway, I've posted this great fall outfit, which I'm hoping to make ASAP and wear to our next Fashion Fun Club meeting. (Although I still haven't figured out how to knit a complete sweater, to be honest, so I'll just start with the shorts.) Anyhoo, the first FFC meeting went really well, although I think a few people in the club weren't quite sure what they were in for . . . and that includes me! But we'll know for next time! I have to come up with next week's activity for the club, so post your ideas in the comments and help me out, pretty please? *Sew long!*

After school the next day, Zoey decided to reach out to one of her "connections," as Ivy called them, and picked up her phone to call her favorite fabric store, and the domain of one of her most trusted sewing advisers.

The store's owner, Jan, answered cheerily, as she always did. "A Stitch in Time, how may I help you?"

"Hi, Jan, it's Zoey." Zoey sat down at her kitchen table and started unloading her books. She had tons of homework to get through.

"Zoey! It's so good to hear from you. But why are you calling me and not here shopping for goodies?"

"Well, I was hoping I could ask you for a favor. I've started a fashion club at my middle school with some other kids, and we need fabric for projects. We have some money from dues, but not a lot, so I was wondering if you have anything discounted we could buy, or if you have any sales coming up, or if you could consider—"

Jan immediately cut her off. "Zoey Webber, I can do better than *that* for one of my favorite customers. I need to clean out my storeroom to make space for new inventory, so I'll just pack up a few boxes of remnants and send them over to your school. Free of charge. How's that?"

Zoey couldn't believe it. She really did have connections! Free fabric for their club! "Oh, Jan, thank you! Thank you a million times. I'm going to make you something verrrrry special in return!"

Jan laughed. "No need. I read your blog last night—I know you're currently designing something very special for Sonya Turley. Congratulations! I'm a huge fan of figure skating, so I'll be watching the nationals in a few weeks, and I'll definitely be cheering for Sonya . . . and your outfit."

"Thanks, Jan! That means so much. And the club will be so happy to have the fabric. We'll put it to good use, I promise!"

"I know you will. Keep creating, Zoey. Just talking to you makes me feel younger and peppier. I might go clean out that storeroom right now!"

Zoey laughed, and she and Jan hung up. Zoey got up to make herself some peanut butter crackers and pour a glass of milk. She was going to need the energy. After she got her homework done, she needed to sit down with Sonya's dress sketch and make some changes the seamstress had asked for.

Zoey knew the client was always right, but it was hard to give up control of the design she loved so much. Luckily, the changes were small, but still . . . . Zoey wanted her nationals debut to be perfect, and it wasn't easy leaving the sewing and final design approval up to someone else!

Most Friday nights, Zoey and her friends tried to get together to do something fun. It didn't always work out, because sometimes Kate had sports practice, and sometimes Libby had ballet, and sometimes Priti had to spend time with her sisters and whichever parent she was staying with that night. But when they did manage to get all four of them together, it was always fun.

Libby had decided they needed a movie night, so the four girls met at their local cinema for one of those movies that parodies everything else that had come out that year.

"Yay!" Libby said as Priti hopped out of her mother's car and came running up to meet her, Zoey, and Kate. "Everybody made it!"

Priti sighed audibly as she joined the girls. "I'm

glad to see you guys. My mom is going to the movies tonight too with some friends, but I convinced her to go to a different theater. Can you *imagine*?"

The girls all laughed, and Zoey handed Priti a box of her favorite sour candies. The girls had already bought popcorn and candy for the group while they waited. Priti thanked her and opened the box immediately.

"Let's go in now so we can get seats together," said Kate, who was wearing a rather adventurous outfit for her. Instead of her usual comfy jeans, she wore a long-sleeve T-shirt dress over a pair of tights with flats. For anyone else, it would just be a cute outfit, but for Kate, it was very girly and fashion-y.

"What's going on, Kate?" Zoey asked. "I didn't even know you owned tights!"

Kate blushed. "Of course I own tights, Zoey. Everyone owns tights."

"You look great," Libby said quickly. "You didn't wear that to school today, though. Is something going on?"

Kate's cheeks grew even redder. "No, I just put

this on because I was meeting you guys. Sheesh! I didn't know I'd be grilled about it."

Sensing Kate's discomfort, Priti interjected. "So, I've decided to stick with volunteering at the home for the elderly. How about you guys? Have you decided on where you'll be doing your twenty hours yet?"

"The food pantry," said Kate, grateful for Priti's help. "There are so many families that just need an extra bag of groceries here and there, and the food pantry makes sure they get it."

"I'm sticking with the animal shelter," said Libby. "Although it'll be hard not to bring them all home! Some of those pups are so sweet."

"How about you, Zoey?" asked Priti. "You're sticking with the thrift store, right? So much great vintage inspiration."

Zoey shook her head. "No, but I thought about it. The store was nice, but they didn't really *need* me. And if the point of this is to help places that need our energy and talents, then I think the pet shelter is better for me. Those sweet animals need love! And maybe Libby and I can even help find some of them forever homes."

Libby clapped her hands and then hugged Zoey. "Yay! You're staying at the shelter with me. I'm so glad."

Priti looked surprised. "Wow, Zoey! I thought for sure you'd stay at the thrift shop. It's so *you*."

"I think you're making a good choice," said Kate. "Those animals need you!"

Zoey grinned. "Well, I have to admit, part of me just likes taking a break from clothes and playing with kittens and puppies for a few hours!"

The girls laughed.

Kate linked her arm through Priti's as they headed into the theater. "So tell us about the home for the elderly, Priti. What do you do there?"

"Well, I read to people and take the library cart around, and I play checkers and just try to be cheerful and friendly to everyone."

"I think it would be hard to be there," says Zoey. "Is it depressing at all?"

"Well, a little bit. Sometimes. But it helps me, you know? It distracts me from thinking about my parents' divorce." She cleared her throat. "You know who else is helping there, by the way? *Ivy.*"

Zoey's jaw dropped. "*Ivy?* Seriously? Is she trying to make the older people feel worse?"

Priti shook her head. "Surprisingly, no. I think I actually saw her smiling and talking nicely to someone the other day. And her grandmother lives there. So maybe she likes to go and visit her, too."

"That's probably what it is," said Libby. "She's not really volunteering; she's just pretending to but visiting her grandmother."

Priti shook her head. "Nope—we all have to do rounds. She can't just stay with one person."

"You should have heard her taunting me in fashion club the other day," said Zoey. "*Ugh.*"

The lights began to dim, and the music for the previews came on. "I don't get it," Kate whispered. "Why would she join the club if she dislikes you and your clothes so much?"

"She didn't know I was in it," Zoey replied. "And now that she does, she'll probably stay just to make me miserable, since that's one of her favorite activities. In any case, I said anyone can join, so I have to let her."

"I'm sorry, Zoey," said Kate. "Let's hope she starts behaving better soon, so she doesn't ruin it for everyone!"

Zoey chuckled. "That's like 'hoping for water in the desert,' as my dad likes to say. *Not* going to happen."

------- CHAPTER 7 -------

Raining Cats and Dogs!

Ack! It's Tuesday again. I went to the pet shelter again over the weekend with my friend, and we had such a great time! The manager let us take a few doggies for a walk after it stopped raining, and we managed to keep them out of the puddles. Then we cleaned cages again, brushed a bunch of the animals, and finally had some great playtime! I'm so relaxed when I'm there, even though I'm "working." I've heard that pets are good for their owners because they lower their heart rates. Do you think that might convince my dad to let us get a dog?

If it doesn't, maybe this sketch will. I got the idea for this cats-and-dogs outfit, and decided to make an "owner outfit" to go along with it. There's just something fantastic about a pet all dressed up. . . . I should dig up some designs from my Doggie Duds line, because my new friends at the shelter might be more adoptable if they had some spiffy clothes. Maybe I can make outfits for a few of them!

I've been working hard at modifying the design for Sonya Turley's skating costume. It turns out that skating costumes have a lot of requirements, including that skaters risk a deduction if a piece of their costume falls onto the ice surface and that the costumes must be considered "modest, appropriate for athletic competition, and not excessively theatrical." Sonya's costumer has been helping me ensure that the design is up to the International Skating Union (ISU) standards.

Who knew, right? Mixing fashion and ice-skating is more complicated than I thought!

I'm sad I won't be making the outfit myself, because I'd love to play with the gorgeous, glitzy fabric they plan to use. I guess I'll have to settle for seeing it on TV! (Although that's not exactly "settling," is it?)☺

Zoey was working hard on a new project in home ec class. It was the pair of pleated, cuffed wool shorts she'd sketched the week before, and she hoped to have it finished for the next fashion club meeting. Mrs. Holmes had assigned everyone the task of completing something with pleats, and Zoey had chosen her shorts. She liked that Mrs. Holmes didn't always dictate exactly what they had to create; she gave them some room to do what interested them.

Priti was making a skirt with pleated detailing, and she was struggling to get her material pinned properly. Occasionally, Zoey would stop and help her, but Priti sometimes insisted Zoey *not* help, so that she could learn to do it herself. Priti had joined home ec because of the cooking component, but she'd come to enjoy the sewing part as well.

When the bell rang signaling the end of the period, Zoey folded up her shorts and placed them in her backpack to take home and finish that night. She still needed to brainstorm activities for tomorrow's fashion club meeting as well. As she and Priti began to clean up their worktable, Mrs. Holmes came by and placed a hand on Zoey's shoulder.

"Zoey, can you stay for a minute after class, please?"

"Oh, sure." Zoey said good-bye to Priti and headed up to the front of the room. Sean was there as well, so Zoey figured it was a safe bet Mrs. Holmes wanted to talk about the fashion club.

Mrs. Holmes pointed to several large cardboard boxes stacked beside her desk. "They're not as heavy they look, but I'm dying to know what's inside. They're all addressed to you, Zoey, care of the Fashion Fun Club!"

"Are they what I think they are?" asked Sean. "Open them!"

Zoey and Sean exchanged excited looks, and Zoey picked up a pair of scissors to begin cutting the tape at the top. Sean helped peel it off, and together they opened the first box.

Inside, it was stuffed to the gills with bolts and bolts of brightly colored fleece in shades of neon yellow, green, and orange. In the next box they found some remnants of plaid flannel, some basic striped cotton, and another bolt of fleece. And the third box held several skeins of neon yarn, and a bag marked "Notions," which Sean picked up.

"Go ahead, look!" Zoey directed.

He opened it to find some ribbon, buttons, and zippers to use for projects. "This is amazing, Zoey! I can't believe you got us all of this. And for free!"

Taped to the side of the third box was a note.

Dearest Zoey,

Hope you can make good use of these materials. Knowing you, you'll find a way to turn lemons into lemonade.

Fondly,

Jan

"Wow, it really is very generous of A Stitch in Time," said Mrs. Holmes. "Now you just need to decide on some projects for your club!"

"What can we make with a bajillion yards of neon fleece?" Sean wondered aloud. "Sleeping bags?"

Zoey laughed. "That would be a riot! Fashionable sleeping bags." She thought a moment. "Fleece jackets seem a little obvious, and the colors are *so* bright, no one would probably wear them. Plus, they might be too difficult to make for beginners. Hmm..."

Mrs. Holmes stayed quiet, watching her students brainstorm.

"Hey, I know!" said Sean. "How about scarves? We could make them reversible, with a different color on each side!"

"Brilliant!" exclaimed Zoey. "That's perfect! Not to mention pretty easy to sew for people who are just getting started. Think how cute and cheerful everyone will look with their neon scarves."

Zoey picked up one of the skeins of yarn, turning it over and over in her hands.

She then held it up to show Sean and Mrs.

Holmes. "You know, I've been trying to learn to knit and watching a lot of online videos about it. The other day I saw this one where someone was making pompoms using yarn and a *fork*. It was really neat, and totally easy. I wonder if we could make pompoms for the ends of our scarves?"

Mrs. Holmes clapped her hands. "What a great team the two of you are! I'm impressed. This club is in good hands—I probably don't even need to show up." She laughed.

Sean grinned. "I think we've found our activity for tomorrow's meeting, Zoey! See? It wasn't that hard, was it?"

Sean and Zoey practiced making the pompoms at the end of lunch period, and as the video promised, it was easy. Zoey was incredibly relieved to have a fun project for the group to do and even more relieved she wouldn't have to think of another project for two more weeks, since next week would be Sean's turn!

At school the next day, she planned to get a bunch of plastic forks from the cafeteria at lunchtime to use for the club. But then she heard a rumor there would be a pop quiz in social studies, so she ended up studying in the library all through lunch and forgot. So by the time the dismissal bell rang, Zoey still had no forks and found herself running to the cafeteria, asking one of the workers to let her into the back area to take a bunch of forks, and dashing down the hall to get to the club meeting.

She arrived breathless and sweaty, and was chagrined to see Ivy already there, sitting serenely at the large table, her lip gloss recently touched up and her mouth in a sneer.

"Sorry I'm late," Zoey sputtered. "I forgot the forks."

Sean shrugged, but everyone was sitting down and waiting on Zoey, who was leading that day's meeting. Sean had gotten out the boxes of fabric for her, and everyone in the room was eyeing them curiously, especially the flap of neon green poking out the top of one.

"Anyone have dues for me today?" Zoey asked hopefully. Sarah passed up money, and Zoey put it into the envelope. She wished the others had remembered as well so she wouldn't have to keep asking! "Let's get started," Zoey continued. She gestured to the boxes of fabric. "As you can see, thanks to the generosity of A Stitch in Time, we have lots of materials!" She showed the fabrics and notions Jan had sent over to the group. Most were pleased, but Ivy, as Zoey had predicted, was less than impressed.

"You can't be serious. What are we going to make with that *hideous* fleece?" Ivy asked.

Zoey and Sean looked at each other. Zoey could feel her resolve to be polite and welcoming to Ivy melting. She forced herself to stay positive.

"We're going to make two-tone reversible scarves," Zoey said evenly, "with pompoms. I know this neat way to make them by hand using a fork. I promise, you guys will love it . . . or at least have fun making them."

Josie smiled, as did Sarah and Emily. Scott, a friend of Sean's from musical theater club, also looked excited.

"Here, let me show you how it works." Zoey quickly got busy using the fork and some of the yarn, weaving the yarn around and through the tines to make a perfect pompom. "Isn't that neat? I think they'll look great on the scarves."

Ivy sighed loudly. "The word 'fashion' shouldn't even be in the name of this club. Not with those fabrics. I'm not making, or wearing, *anything* made of that stuff."

Zoey gritted her teeth and was relieved when Sean spoke up, keeping his tone light and jokey. "If you're not into scarves, Ivy, you could try a pillow with pompoms around the edges. It would be really soft in the fleece, and you could stuff it using an old pillow from home." He handed her a fork and some of the yarn, almost daring her to try making a pompom.

Sean seemed to have the magic touch with Ivy, because she stopped hissing and reluctantly agreed to try it. Her fingers began working with the yarn and fork, and it seemed to calm her down to be busy.

The rest of the club got to work choosing and pinning fabric, and making pompoms. Zoey started having fun when she saw how much the other kids were enjoying the project, and she got up and went over to Sean, who was collecting pins for everyone to use.

"She's awful, isn't she?" Zoey whispered. "And she's been like that forever. She'll never change."

Sean half nodded, but then stopped himself. "You know, I think she's just uptight. She has to say a few mean things when she first arrives, to get comfortable, and then she sort of relaxes and chills out. It's more like she's really insecure rather than just evil."

Zoey wasn't buying it. "But then why are the mean things always directed at *me*?"

Sean smiled and patted Zoey on the back. "Because you're so together, Zoey. And deep down, Ivy knows she's not. Remember, if she didn't want to be here, she wouldn't have come back. And she *did* actually pay her dues."

Zoey thought Sean was deluding himself, but she admired how mature he was about a person coming in and being a jerk in their club. He acted like it was no big deal and just stayed pleasant and cheerful, running around the room helping everyone.

Sean Waschikowsi was a good guy.

Many of the club members stayed late that day to finish their scarves. Sean got really into it and ended up taking some contrasting thread and embroidering *FFC* on the bottom of his scarf. As soon as the rest of the club members saw that, they wanted letters on theirs too. So Sean gave everyone a quick lesson on how to embroider letters in backstitch.

Everyone except Ivy, who was the only one working on a pillow, thanked Sean for the lesson and quickly got to work embroidering their own letters.

"Thank you for showing us that!" Josie said to Sean. "I've always wanted to make handkerchiefs and embroider my initials on them. I can't wait to try it now!"

Sean waved his hand, like it was no big deal. But Zoey could tell how impressed the club was with his skills.

After another fifteen minutes or so, the group began to clean up and put away their materials so they could head outside to catch the late bus home. As they were leaving, Gabe asked everyone if they could huddle together for a minute in their scarves, so he could take a group picture.

"It'd be great for the school paper," Gabe explained. "Or the yearbook."

Everyone wrapped their new scarves, some with half-finished letters on them, around their necks and struck a pose. Ivy stood off to the side, holding her pillow in front of her like a shield.

"Squeeze in, Ivy, I can only see your shoulder," Gabe directed.

Ivy did as she was told, although Zoey thought the expression on Ivy's face made it look like it was the *last* place Ivy wanted to be. Gabe took a few shots and promised to e-mail the best one to the group.

"Thank you, Gabe," Mrs. Holmes said as the rest of the group began to depart to get in line for the late bus. "Please send me a copy as well. I have a feeling this is going to be a very special group."

She winked at Zoey and Sean, then locked the classroom door behind her and left for the faculty parking lot.

Gabe waved good-bye as well. "I've got to get

something from my locker real quick. See you guys in the bus line!"

Zoey and Sean headed down the empty hall together, recapping their meeting.

Sean said, "You know, I bet Ivy wants a scarf now, since everyone else has one. She looked sort of odd standing there with her pillow in the picture. But I bet she'd be too embarrassed to say so since she was so negative about the scarves earlier."

Zoey couldn't help replying, "Good, I hope she feels left out again when we're all wearing our scarves tomorrow."

"*Zoey.*"

"I know that was awful. I'm sorry, but she brings it out in me." Zoey felt guilty immediately and then reminded herself for what felt like the hundredth time that she had promised to be welcoming to Ivy. It was just so *hard* to forget all the mean things Ivy had done to her in the past. "I'll try to be better—I promise."

Sean waited a beat, then said, "Aw, don't beat yourself up too much, Zoey. That girl can be a real jerk sometimes."

Zoey laughed and threw her arms around Sean. "Thank you for saying that, Sean. If even *you*—patient, perfect *you*—think that, then maybe I'm not such a terrible person after all."

"You're *sew* not terrible." He grinned. "I've just been teased so much about my sewing and interest in fashion that I've decided to always be extra careful about the way *I* treat people. Being nice isn't that hard, you know."

"You're right," Zoey agreed. "And it's especially easy to be nice to *you*."

"Why, thank you, Madame Vice President. Now, we'd better hurry, or we're going to miss the bus!"

CHAPTER 8

Pompom-*Mania*!

If you haven't made a pompom with yarn and a fork, try it. It's addictive! You can find a how-to video online, and in five minutes, you'll be making so many pompoms you won't know what to do with them all. Hence (don't you love that word?), this darling pompom dress in a cozy flannel, inspired by the flannel remnants that were donated to the Fashion Fun Club. It would be great with tights and boots on cold days!

The Fashion Fun Club displayed some awesome club spirit today by wearing the new neon scarves (*avec* pompoms!) that we made yesterday. Sean taught us how to embroider them with the letters *FFC* and you should have seen how proud everyone was of our new club!

In other news, I sent off the final, final design sketch to Sonya Turley's costumer, and I expect to get a photo of the actual, completed outfit in just a few days! I can't believe how fast a professional costumer works. But I guess she has to, since Sonya will be competing at nationals in just two weeks, and the outfit must be ready. Come to think of it, my new flannel pompom dress would be the perfect warm and cozy thing to wear while *watching* ice-skating live at a rink! For this competition, though, I'll be watching from the comfort of my own living room. Maybe next time!☺

"Wait, wait, wait," Priti exclaimed. "A boy *what*?"

"Shh!" Kate immediately turned bright red and

waved her hands frantically at Priti to quiet her. Zoey and her friends were sitting at their usual table in the lunchroom, and there was very little privacy with a hundred or so other middle schoolers jammed in around them.

"Okay, I'll *whisper*, but you need to tell us every detail *from the beginning*," Priti urged. The girls hunched over their lunches, so their faces were closer together.

"We look like we're plotting," Libby joked.

"Maybe we are," Priti replied.

Kate sighed, and began her story again. "So, there's this boy Tyler who volunteers at the food pantry with me, and he's fourteen, and a freshman in high school. And he's very nice, and we've been talking a lot while we're there. And yesterday he asked me to go out *on a date*."

Zoey shook her head. She couldn't believe it. Shy Kate, who barely noticed boys and usually only thought of them as potential athletic opponents, had been asked out by a high school boy!

"What did you say?" asked Zoey. "Did you turn as red as you are right now?"

"Ha-ha, Zoey," said Kate. "And yes, I probably did. I said, 'Um, I don't know,' because I *don't* know! Help, you guys, I need advice!"

"Advice? Just go, and have fun!" Priti shook her head, as if Kate was delusional.

Kate bit her lip. "I'm kind of weirded out by the whole idea of a real date. I mean, Tyler's in high school. I've never even thought about going on a date. What would we do?"

"Don't worry about that part yet," Libby advised. "Do you like him? That's the most important thing."

"I think he's nice," said Kate. "I don't know him very well."

"What would you wear?" Zoey mused. "Hmm, you looked really cute last weekend in that T-shirt dress and tights. You could wear that!"

Kate laughed. "I don't need to worry about my outfit yet, Zoey. I don't even know if I'm actually going to *go*!"

Zoey smiled. Then she asked, somewhat hesitantly, "What about Lorenzo?"

Lorenzo Romy was a boy who had liked Kate a while back, and even though Zoey had kind of liked him herself once, she'd realized he was only interested in Kate. So Zoey had told Kate to go for it, but Kate never had.

"We're just friends," Kate replied. "Anyway, I heard he's seeing this girl Mira from the soccer team."

"Hmm," said Priti, finally opening her lunch and biting into her sandwich. "I think it'd be silly to say no when you could go out and have a really good time. And if you don't have a good time, you can always say no the next time."

"Let's change the subject," Kate said. "I've been worrying about it all morning! Somebody talk about something else, please."

Libby, always the most sensitive to other's feelings, quickly jumped in. "What do you guys think those bright neon scarves are for? Have you seen them?" The girls turned their heads, and it was easy to pick out the scarves in the cafeteria. They practically glowed under the fluorescent lights.

Zoey laughed. "You haven't been reading my blog, Libby!" she said, pretending to scold her friend. "We made them in the Fashion Fun Club this week."

"I love them," Priti said. "I want one! But where is yours, Zoey?"

Embarrassed, Zoey shrugged. She'd forgotten hers at home that morning. "It didn't go with my outfit today. That, and I forgot to bring it!"

As if on cue, Ivy strolled by Zoey's table and said, "Not wearing your scarf, Zoey? It's because you *know* that neon is hideous. And now everyone else is stuck wearing them! Good one." She shook her head and then headed to her table by the front to join her friends Shannon Chang and Bree Sharpe.

Zoey rolled her eyes as her friends looked at her sympathetically.

"She's really improved," Priti said sarcastically.

"Is she making the fashion club awful?" asked Libby.

"*Yeeeees*," moaned Zoey. "At least for me. I mean, it's fun, and I like talking about fashion stuff with everyone, but it's a lot more work than I thought it would be. I have to come up with activities, collect dues, deal with Ivy, and teach people how to do stuff."

"It'll get easier," said Kate. "Every season, when soccer or swimming starts, and I begin the work-outs after having a break, I think that I won't make the team, that I'm not as strong as I need to be, you know. But then I get used to it and get better and start having fun again! You just have to stick with it through the hard, beginning part."

Zoey mulled that over. Maybe the club would get easier once it wasn't so new. She vowed to give it her best effort and hope that Kate was right.

"Not that I don't *love* talking about Ivy," said Priti, "but can we talk about this Tyler a little more? What's he like, Kate?"

Kate and Zoey looked at each other and smiled. Despite having had a hard few months at home after her parents split up, and totally changing her wardrobe to mostly black or dark-colored clothing, Priti was the same old Priti. Enthusiastic and just a little bit boy-crazy.

"Well, I have a picture," Kate admitted reluc-tantly. She pulled her cell phone from her pocket and held it up to show a photo of Tyler with some of the other volunteers from the food pantry.

"Oooh, he is cute!" Libby said. "Say yes, Kate. C'mon!"

Kate put away her phone and sighed. "He is, but I don't think we have very much in common. He doesn't play any sports, and that's, you know, a big deal to me. What would we talk about on a date?"

Libby grinned. "The four of us hardly ever talk about sports, and you still like all of us!"

Kate laughed, and so did the rest of the group.

"Boys will do a lot for love," Priti said knowingly. "Maybe he'll turn out to be an athlete just to prove his feelings for you!"

Libby shook her head. "Even if he *doesn't*, my mom says opposites attract for a reason. It would be boring for Kate to date someone exactly like her!"

Instead of getting the joke, Kate's face immediately fell.

Libby instantly understood her statement had been misinterpreted, and she grabbed Kate's arm. "No! Kate, I didn't mean that *you* are boring. Just that it's more interesting to hang out with people who are different from us!"

"I get it," Kate said. "I see what you mean."

"Listen, Kate," said Priti. "I know I'm being sort of a hypocrite, because I don't go out with every boy who asks me out, but I really think you should give this guy a shot. He sounds sweet, and he's a little older, so he's probably more mature than the guys in our grade. What do you have to lose?"

"Nothing, I guess," Kate admitted. "But I'm still not ready to decide."

"Take your time," Zoey advised. "You won't see him for another few days, right? So you can think about it. And then say yes."

"Maybe," agreed Kate.

"*Yes*," said Priti.

"*Maybe*," Kate repeated with a smile.

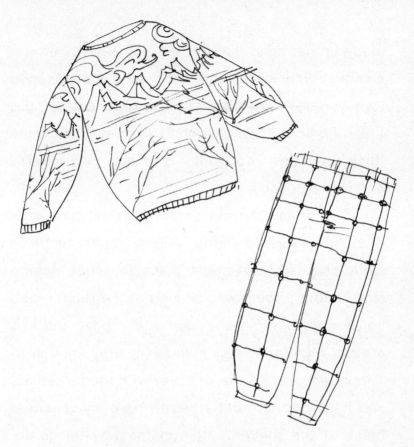

CHAPTER 9

Not in My Nature!

Oh readers! Why is life *sew* complicated?

I was chatting with some friends about whether or not one friend should say yes to an invitation. And she was very hesitant about it and didn't know what to do. And I think it was partly because she had already made up her mind that the she didn't have much in common with the person who issued the invitation (can you tell how hard I'm trying to protect this friend's privacy? Cryptic, right?). Anyway, it made me think about how important it is to stay open-minded and try new things!

Like me and the pet shelter. One of my friends thought for *sure* I'd end up volunteering at the thrift store because it's a great place to scout vintage clothes. But playing with animals at the shelter is so much more fun to me! I went again today and had a blast. My brother's girlfriend was lucky enough to adopt two cats, so she can play with them anytime, and I'm so jealous! But at least I have my volunteer hours at the shelter, and with the way things are going, I'll end up with way more than the twenty-hour minimum I need.

And speaking of being open-minded, check out my sketch! I love the mix of patterned pants with a shirt screenprinted with a nature pic. Maybe it's not in everyone's *nature* to mix prints and graphics, but it's worth a try. It's unexpected and fun!

Zoey looked forward to her family's Sunday breakfast every week, and since Aunt Lulu had married John, they'd been coming by as well to join the fun. Lulu always referred to it as "brunch," which Zoey liked, and this week, Zoey and Marcus had decided to fully initiate their new uncle John into the family by allowing him to make the secret-ingredient pancakes.

Normally, the family hung out together at the kitchen table while the pancakes were made, and they simply turned their heads while the designated chef added the secret ingredient(s). But Uncle John was taking his job very seriously.

"Everyone into the living room, please," he said as he tied on an apron he'd brought from home. "I need quiet to make my magic."

"It's just pancake mix," said Marcus. "And some eggs. And a hot pan."

Uncle John shook his head. "No, Marcus. It's much, much more."

Aunt Lulu beamed at him and then blew him a kiss before heading into the living room with Zoey, Marcus, and Mr. Webber. They all sat down to chat.

"How's the outfit for Sonya Turley?" Lulu asked Zoey. "Have you seen a photo yet?"

"Almost done, I think," Zoey replied. "The costumer is going to send me a picture when it's ready. I can't wait to see it on Sonya, though, moving across the ice!"

"Me too," said Aunt Lulu. "What an opportunity for you! When I die, I want to come back as you."

Zoey laughed. She wouldn't mind coming back as her aunt, who ran a successful interior design business, had a wonderful dog, and now a wonderful husband, as well.

"How are Allie's new cats?" Zoey asked her brother. She'd been meaning to go over to Allie's house and visit them, but with the fashion club and volunteering at the shelter, her schedule was pretty full.

"They're great. They've adapted really well to their new home, and Allie says they've become like mother and son, kind of, even though they aren't. They curl up together and sleep!"

Zoey smiled and made up her mind that she would go and visit immediately.

"That's pretty cute," Mr. Webber admitted. "And

I'm not a cat person at all. Where is Allie this morning, Marcus? She's certainly welcome to join us."

Marcus looked at his knees, which jutted out in front of him on the couch. "She and I are kind of in a fight. A small fight." He cleared his throat in an odd way and then said, "Anyway, that's why she didn't come over."

"Oh, Marcus, I'm sorry," Lulu said quickly.

"If it's truly something small, just go ahead and say you're sorry, kiddo," Mr. Webber said. "Whatever it is, it's probably not worth fighting over."

Marcus's face was slowly turning beet red. Zoey knew how much Marcus disliked the family interfering in his personal life, and even though Allie had been Zoey's friend to begin with—and, therefore, Zoey felt she was owed more of an explanation—she decided to help out her brother by taking the focus off him.

"Ugh! I almost forgot," Zoey said loudly. "Did you bring any towels for the shelter, Aunt Lulu?"

Lulu nodded and tipped her head toward the front hall, to indicate she'd left them there. "We got a bunch of new ones for wedding presents, so I brought you our old ones."

"What's this for again, Zoey?" Mr. Webber asked. "I saw you going through the linen closet earlier and meant to ask."

"The shelter. They go through tons of towels, so I'm trying to help collect some to donate."

Zoey went to check the bag that Lulu had brought, putting it next to the bag of old towels she'd pulled from the linen closet. Even with two full bags, it didn't seem like enough. Not with new animals coming and going at the shelter all the time.

Suddenly, an idea hit Zoey. A *bright* idea! The neon fleece Jan had donated to the fashion club would be perfect to turn into cuddly towels for the animals. And it would make a terrific next project for the club meeting! Zoey couldn't wait to tell Sean and the rest of the FFC. If they could sew something and help out some animals in need at the same time, it would be a win-win!

Uncle John appeared from the kitchen, his apron streaked with gooey batter, carrying a platter piled high with delicious-smelling pancakes.

"Breakfast is served," he said, gesturing with his arm for them to all head into the kitchen to eat. As usual, the dining room was completely taken over by Zoey's sewing machine, materials, and current projects. Luckily, the Webbers had a sunny eating space in the kitchen.

The family filed in and took their seats. Uncle John dished out the pancakes, passed the syrup, and waited anxiously.

Aunt Lulu was the first taster. She cut herself a generous piece and then popped it in her mouth. "Mmm," she said. "Chewy and delicious."

Chewy? Zoey had never heard pancakes described as *chewy*. She hurriedly cut a few pieces from her own stack and took a bite. They *were* chewy! They were thicker than usual, and had a soft texture, too. Zoey couldn't put her finger on the flavor, though.

"Banana!" Marcus said immediately, his mouth full. "But you chopped it up really tiny so we couldn't guess it. And the chewy part is . . ." He thought a moment and continued to chew.

Zoey took another bite, as did her father. They all chewed silently for a moment while Uncle John smiled, pleased that he had stumped them.

Mr. Webber smacked his hand on the table.

"I've got it," he said. "Granola. I just got a chunk. Delicious, John!"

Aunt Lulu shook her head. "Granola in pancakes? Who would think of that but you?" She leaned toward John and gave him a quick kiss, right at the breakfast table. Marcus took another helping of pancakes and ate enthusiastically, his fight with Allie temporarily forgotten.

Zoey looked around the table, thinking to herself how much she loved Sundays. A whole day of the week devoted to just family and sewing. What could be better?

Zoey couldn't wait to share her idea to make towels for the animal shelter. She made sure she got to home ec class a few minutes early on Monday morning, to discuss it with Sean. Unfortunately, when she arrived, he was already talking to Emily and Ivy. She noticed that Emily and Sean were both wearing their scarves, and Zoey realized she'd forgotten hers yet again.

"H-hi, guys," Zoey said, stumbling over her words. She didn't want to mention her idea in front of Ivy. She knew Ivy would shoot it down as silly or ridiculous or tacky. Or possibly all three.

"Sean, can I talk to you for second?" Zoey said. "I have an idea for a club activity."

Sean smiled, his grin wide and easy. "Sure, Zoey! Let's hear it." But he made no move to step away from Emily and Ivy. In fact, the two girls leaned in closer toward Zoey, as if they too, wanted to hear it.

Zoey was stuck. Now she'd have to tell them and risk getting more of Ivy's comments in return. Luckily, at that moment, Priti walked into the classroom and came over to stand by Zoey.

"Morning, everyone," Priti said cheerily. "What's going on?"

Zoey wasn't sure if Priti sensed that Zoey needed some backup or was just curious about the huddle they all stood in.

"Zoey was just about to wow us with her idea for a fashion project," Emily said.

Zoey had no choice now. She had to tell them. "Well, um, we still have all that fleece, and I know not everyone loves the colors. The pet shelter where I'm volunteering really needs extra towels for the dogs and cats to snuggle with, so I thought we could make them some fleece blankets. It'd be a really easy sewing project, and we'd be doing something helpful for the community, too."

"Sounds perfect!" Priti said loudly, and Zoey knew then that Priti *had* deliberately come and stood there to help her. She made a mental note to thank Priti later.

Sean nodded vigorously. "That's a great idea. It's not exactly fashion related, but it does involve sewing, and I think it would be great if the club can help out those animals."

Zoey had been pretty sure Sean would approve, so she continued to hold her breath, waiting to hear what Ivy's reaction would be.

She was amazed when Ivy tossed her hair back and said, "You know, the residents at the senior home where *I'm* volunteering could really use some blankets. A lot of the folks are in wheelchairs and get cold really easily, and the fleece would be great for that."

"You're so thoughtful!" Emily exclaimed, like Ivy had had the idea to use the fabric to help those in their community service projects first.

"That's a great idea too, Ivy!" Sean said warmly. Zoey could tell he was trying to reward Ivy for being nice, in the hopes that the good behavior would continue. "We can have everyone make a towel *and* a blanket for our activity this week. Neither require any difficult sewing."

Zoey was annoyed. Yes, Ivy had managed not to shoot down or insult Zoey's idea, per se, but she'd also managed to make it feel less special by adding her own project on top of it.

Then, to Zoey's total amazement, Priti said, "You're right, Ivy, a lot of the residents often do complain about being cold. Fleece blankets would be perfect. And the neon is cheerful!"

Mrs. Holmes came in to start class, and Zoey and Priti moved over to their table.

Zoey couldn't help whispering, "Uh, excuse me? Did you just compliment *Ivy* on her idea?"

Priti shrugged. "I know it sounds crazy, but I'm with her at the senior center every week, and she's actually pretty good with the elderly. I've seen her being really nice."

"Not to *me*," Zoey reminded her.

"No, not to you," Priti agreed. "But just think about how happy you guys will make all those old people and puppies with your projects. That's worth ignoring Ivy for, I think."

Reluctantly, Zoey had to agree. It was more important to make the blankets than it was to prove that Ivy was still vicious at heart. Zoey would try to rise above Ivy, once again.

When Zoey got home that afternoon, she was thrilled to find a smallish brown box on her front porch. Brown boxes were usually either fabric she'd ordered online or surprises from Daphne Shaw, her not-so-secret-anymore fashion fairy godmother–turned-mentor. When she checked the return address, she was delighted to see it *was* from Daphne. Eagerly, she used her house key to cut through the brown packing tape to see what Daphne had sent her.

Inside, she found a pile of brightly colored silicone bracelets, all stamped with the words "Fashion Fun Club." Zoey couldn't believe it! What a neat idea, and something she knew the other members of the club would love. She sifted through the bracelets until she found a small, folded piece of white paper. She opened it and read:

Dear Zoey,
   I'm so proud of you for starting a fashion club at your middle school! I wish we had had one when I was in school. Make sure you keep the "Fun" in the club, because after all, that's what clubs are for. Hope the other members know how lucky they are to have you!
   Your friend,
   Daphne Shaw

Zoey slid one of the bracelets onto her arm. She couldn't help thinking that while the words "fun" and "fashion" went together like peanut butter and jelly, the words "fun" and "Ivy" had no business being in the same club. At least, not to Zoey.

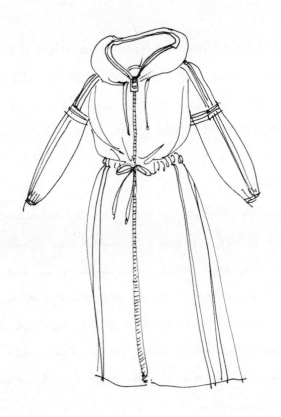

------- CHAPTER 10 -------

Wowable Warm-Ups!

The Fashion Fun Club met today and began work on making towels for the animals at the shelter and blankets for the elderly at the senior home. S and I did a lot of troubleshooting with people's sewing machines, so I didn't get to sew much myself ☺, but there's always next week! And I gave out the personalized silicone bracelets that my always-generous fashion mentor (who shall still remain nameless!) sent us. The club didn't seem as excited as I thought they'd be to have a gift from an anonymous famous designer, and one person **in particular** mentioned they were hoping for an invite to a fashion show instead. Sigh. I do plan to bring a bunch of the new towels to the shelter with me next week, so that's something!

Since the theme for this post seems to be helping people (and pets!) stay warm, I posted this sketch of a great athletic warm-up dress I designed for Sonya Turley. Her costumer didn't end up making it, though, because Sonya already has a "lucky" warm up suit that she likes to wear, but she asked to see more of my sketches in the future. Sounds good to me!

After school on Thursday, Zoey found herself walking up the street to Kate's house. Tyler had asked Kate out again while they were volunteering that week, and to everyone's surprise—hers most of all—she'd said yes. Now she desperately needed an outfit to wear on their date, and Zoey had volunteered help pick something out.

Zoey stood at Kate's door with her hand raised, about to knock, when the door swung open. It was Kate, and her cheeks were flushed bright pink.

"I can't believe I said yes," she blurted out. "Now I'm so nervous. I blame Priti!"

Zoey laughed, knowing that Kate was joking. She'd known Kate for most of her life, and though Kate was shy, she wasn't a pushover. You couldn't talk her into something unless she wanted to do it.

Zoey patted Kate's arm and said, "Stop worrying! You'll have fun. It's just for a few hours. Think of him as a friend, not a date."

"Ugh, I suppose so." Kate led Zoey up to her room, where she'd pulled some clothes from her closet and drawers and laid them on her bed.

"This is everything I have that isn't horrible," Kate declared. "Can you make me an actual outfit out of this?"

"You know you can borrow anything of mine that you like, Kate, but let's see what you have here first. Where's that T-shirt dress I liked?" Zoey asked, sifting through the pile of striped T-shirts and V-necks. They were basic clothes that didn't stand out, which is exactly what Kate preferred. Zoey noticed that Kate hadn't pulled any of the floral dresses or patterned skirts from her closet. Those were items that Kate's mom had bought for her, and that Kate rarely wore unless forced to do so.

"I'm *not* wearing a dress," Kate said. "That's too fancy, and he'll think I'm taking the date too seriously. I don't want to look like I'm trying too hard, okay?"

Zoey nodded. "Okay, I understand. And I think you're right to be yourself! But I'm going to make you look like your best self. Your best *comfy* self."

Kate laughed and flopped down on her beanbag chair to watch Zoey work her magic. After just a few minutes, Zoey had pulled together a pink printed tank top, with a fitted teal cardigan, and a pair of boyfriend jeans, with the cuffs rolled.

"The teal looks great with your blond hair, and the little pink tank underneath is feminine, but not too much. And the jeans say comfy, not trying hard. What shoes do you want to wear?"

"My flattest flats," Kate said matter-of-factly. "Tyler's a little shorter than I am, and I don't want to make him feel weird by wearing shoes with thick soles or something."

"Flats are perfect with this. Don't you have a gold pair your mom bought you?"

Kate waved vaguely at her closet. "They're in there somewhere. I've never worn them. Gold is so fancy!"

Zoey couldn't help laughing. "Gold flats are not *fancy*. They're neutral and perfect for this outfit. And you can pair them with one of these cute jackets your mom bought you. . . . But don't forget to take off the price tag!" Kate didn't look convinced, so Zoey continued. "Listen to me, Kate Mackey: You will wear the gold flats and a cute jacket, you will look great, and you will have *fun!*"

Already the nervous look had crept back into Kate's eyes. "If you say so," she said. "But I'm still blaming Priti for this. I'm going to call her and yell at her right now."

"Nooooo . . . you'll be *thanking her* when your date is awesome!" said Zoey.

"I hope so. I really hope so. But that makes me even *more* nervous!"

That night, while Zoey was doing her homework, her phone beeped. She normally turned it off while she was studying, but she was worried Kate might need her for moral support that evening, so she left it on. Zoey put down her social studies book and picked up her phone to read the e-mail.

It was from someone named Tyler Landon.

Dear Zoey,

I found your e-mail address on your blog. I hope you don't mind me e-mailing you! I'm a friend of Kate's, and she talks about you all the time. I'm taking Kate out tomorrow night, and I want to make sure she has a good time on the date. Since you're her best friend, would you mind telling me a few of her favorite things, so I can make sure the date is perfect?

Sincerely,

Tyler Landon

Zoey gulped. Kate's date wanted advice on how to impress her? It was sweet, very sweet, but at the same time, his e-mailing Zoey behind Kate's back felt a little bit sneaky. Like someone with seventh-period social studies asking someone in first-period social studies what questions were on the quiz that morning. Well, technically that was actual cheating, and this was . . . what, exactly? Playing cupid? Or Cyrano de Bergerac, the guy in that French movie they'd watched last semester where one man tells another exactly what to say and do to woo a woman?

Feeling uneasy, Zoey started typing a reply.

Tyler,

Hi! I'm afraid I don't know very much about dating, and I feel a little weird getting involved, honestly! But Kate is a wonderful person, and I think it's nice that you want to impress her. I can tell you that Kate doesn't care much about fancy food or clothes, but she does love sports. She'd probably think it was cool if you showed up in a soccer jersey from her favorite team, or

took her to the batting cages for a date, but you
should just do whatever sounds like fun to you!

Have fun!

Zoey

Zoey hit send, relieved that she'd managed to
both help Tyler, and not reveal anything about
her friend that wasn't already pretty obvious. She
picked up her social studies book and got back to
reading.

She was surprised when a minute later, her
phone beeped again.

Zoey,

Thank you! This is really helpful. I'm terrible
at baseball, but maybe I can practice before I take
her to the batting cages. I wanted to ask you one
more thing . . . I'm not quite as tall as Kate . . . Do
you think that matters to her?

Tyler

Surprised by the question, Zoey wrote back
immediately.

Of course not, Tyler! Kate isn't like that *at all.* She's kind and fun and likes to be around people who are the same. I hope you guys have a terrific time!

Zoey

She waited a minute or two to see if he'd write back, but he didn't. Satisfied she'd done her job, she resolved to finish studying. But a moment later, an idea for a great date outfit came to her, and she picked up her sketchpad to do a quick drawing, making sure to sketch a cute pair of flats to go with it.

CHAPTER 11

A Sneaky Secret

What's that saying again? "Secrets, secrets are no fun. Secrets, secrets hurt someone?" Ugh. I have a little secret myself at the moment, and I *can't* reveal it, and it's starting to make me feel uncomfortable. Readers, is it okay to keep a secret when you're trying to do something nice for a friend? Like, if you're helping someone who wants to make one of your friends happy, but you're not telling the friend about it? I know, it's hard to answer without knowing exactly who I mean. There should be an absolute black-and-white code written somewhere that spells out exactly what you have to reveal and what you don't!

On a related note, I was thinking last night about what kind of outfit would be perfect for a date (not that I'm going on one any time soon . . . unless someone is keeping a secret from *me*!) The ideal outfit needs to be fun, and comfortable, in case you end up going bowling, or playing skee ball, or seeing a movie. But you still want to look cute and girly! I think this design hits it on the nose. Plus, it has a happy heart!

On Saturday morning, Zoey volunteered at the animal shelter with Libby again. Zoey still hadn't heard anything from Kate about her date the night before, so she and Libby hatched a plan for all the girls to meet at their favorite ice cream parlor after they'd finished their volunteer commitments. Libby texted everyone, and Priti and Kate both replied "YES!" almost instantly.

Even though Zoey and Libby both loved being with the animals, the morning felt slower than usual since they were anxious to talk to Kate. When it was finally noon, Zoey and Libby said good-bye to Stephen and went outside, where Mrs. Flynn was waiting to pick them up and drive them to the ice cream parlor.

They arrived just a minute or two late and found Priti already there, saving them a table in the corner. Zoey and Libby offered to get ice cream for everyone and bring it to the table. As soon as they sat down, Kate arrived. Her hair was in a messy ponytail, and she was wearing a US Youth Soccer league T-shirt, a pair of navy Spandex, and sneakers.

"Is *that* what you wore to the food pantry today?" Priti asked. She made a face like she'd tasted something bad. "Was Tyler there?"

Kate raised her eyebrows as she slid into the empty seat with the hot fudge sundae in front of it. "Thanks for the sundae, guys," she said. "And *yes*, Priti, this is what I wore. I help stock shelves and pack bags of groceries. Did you want me to wear a miniskirt?"

"So I guess that means the date didn't go very well," Priti said, getting right to point. She sighed heavily, as if it were her own date that hadn't gone well.

A slow smile crept across Kate's face as she loaded her spoon with ice cream and chocolate sauce. "Actually, it was kind of fun."

"IT WAS?" Zoey, Priti, and Libby screeched at once.

Kate frowned. "*Quiet,*" she said. "This place is packed. Try not to embarrass me, please."

Libby put her hand on Kate's arm. "Tell us everything, Kate. We're all dying to hear! It's the only thing Zoey and I talked about this morning, even though there was a litter of brand-new puppies at the shelter!"

Kate took a slow bite of her sundae just to torture everyone. Zoey couldn't help thinking that even with the old clothes and messy ponytail, Kate was undeniably beautiful. Her high cheekbones, rosy cheeks, and sparkling eyes made her a standout, no matter what she wore.

"Well, we had a good time hanging out, and he said he wants to hang out again soon," Kate said.

"And?" prompted Libby. "Details, please!"

"Um, we went to the batting cages. Then out for pizza. And he wore a soccer jersey, which I liked."

"Sounds like a very Kate date," said Priti. "That means he really gets you."

Zoey couldn't look at Kate. Instead, she focused on her double scoop of Rainbow Delight and pralines 'n' cream. Zoey didn't realize Tyler would take her advice so literally.

"It was very me," Kate admitted. "*But*, I'm sort of conflicted. I felt really comfortable in my outfit, thanks to Zoey, but not so comfortable about the date."

"What do you mean?" asked Libby.

Kate twirled her spoon in the hot fudge. "I don't know. I sort of felt like I was *acting* while I was with him, instead of just being myself. I really don't think I'm old enough to date yet, so I was pretending to be someone who was."

Priti shook her head. "It was only one date. You

might have just been nervous. Did you guys have a lot to talk about?"

"Well, he kept trying to bring up sports, but I could tell he didn't know anything about them, and that was awkward. So I would try to ask him questions about himself and what he liked. I mean, I did laugh a lot, because he's funny and nice. But I was also really relieved when it was time to go home."

Libby asked, "So are you going to go out with him again?"

"I don't know," said Kate. "We'll see. At the food pantry this morning, another volunteer tossed him a bag of rice, and he dropped it. And he looked at me right away—*guiltily*—like I was judging his athletic abilities or something."

"Were you?" Zoey asked. "You're not turning into an Ivy, are you?"

Kate rolled her eyes. "No! But he has no hand-eye coordination. Like, *none*."

"Neither do I!" Zoey exclaimed. "Thank goodness I can sew. I have *needle-eye* coordination."

"Ha-ha," said Kate. "Ew! Or ouch?"

Zoey grinned. It was a good sign that Kate had a sense of humor about it.

"Actually, Ivy has gotten a lot better recently," Priti said. "I can't believe I'm saying that, but you should see her at the nursing home after school. It's like being around older people makes her nicer or something."

"I'll believe it when I see it," said Zoey. "She's still pretty nasty to me."

"I know," Priti said. "I guess I'm just hoping she's improving."

Deep down, Zoey didn't believe Ivy would ever really be nice to her. There was too much history between them.

And Kate? Well, Zoey knew Kate better than anyone—and she could tell that Kate was being pretty close-minded about Tyler. Maybe he didn't have much athletic ability, but that didn't mean he wasn't worth being friends with. Especially since he was making such an effort to please Kate.

Zoey wondered for a moment if she should tell Kate that Tyler liked her so much, he'd e-mailed her best friend for ideas on how to impress her. But she decided not to. Somehow, she knew if she told Kate, Kate would like Tyler even less. And Zoey couldn't help rooting for him a little bit. Any boy that liked her friend enough to take her to the batting cages, when he himself could hardly hit a ball, deserved a second chance. At least in her book.

Ivy, on the other hand, had used up all her second chances. And her third. And even her fourth!

At the next Fashion Fun Club meeting, the group continued to work with the bolts of fleece fabric. Sean had decided to make it a challenge that they use every scrap of it and had asked all the members to come up with unique sewing projects for it. Zoey was happy to let Sean lead the group that day, as her mind was elsewhere. Tyler had e-mailed her again, asking for advice about Kate, and she was having a hard time answering him without feeling like she was betraying her friend, while at the same time hoping Tyler would find a way to get Kate to be more open-minded about him not being athletic. As far as Zoey could tell, Tyler was a really, really nice boy.

"What are you working on, Zoey?" Josie asked,

interrupting Zoey's train of thought.

"Um, I'm not sure yet," Zoey admitted. "You?"

Josie held up the beginning of what looked like a little capelet, which had slit pockets in contrasting fabric on the sides. It was very chic, even in fleece! Zoey was impressed. Mrs. Holmes had given the group some simple patterns from her filing cabinet to use, and everyone was hard at work.

Zoey looked around the rest of the table at the other projects. Emily had decided to make herself a ski hat; a few kids were making zip-up fleece vests, which Mrs. Holmes was helping with by attaching the zippers; and Ivy was making another fleece pillow with pompoms.

"I gave the first pillow I made to my grandmother," Ivy was saying. "And she loves it! She keeps it in her wheelchair for her back, but now she wants another for a bolster for when she's reading in bed. So I'm making this one a little bit bigger."

"How is your grandmother?" Sean asked Ivy nicely. Zoey continued to be amazed by how nice Sean was to Ivy. It was like he'd made it his mission to kill her with kindness. "Maybe she'd like a scarf, too? We have plenty of extra material."

Ivy nodded slowly. "That's a good idea, Sean. Thanks!"

Zoey was almost positive that if *she* had suggested Ivy make a scarf, Ivy would have snapped at Zoey that her grandmother would never wear anything so ugly.

Zoey decided she would experiment with the fleece and try to make flowers with it to attach to a skirt. She wasn't sure it would work, but she didn't feel like sewing that day. She felt like thinking and fiddling.

"You know," Ivy said loudly, to no one in particular, "my little cousin was at the nursing home with me the other day. She's in fifth grade, and— you guys are not even going to believe this—she's being bullied at school."

Sean cocked his head sideways. "Bullied? How?"

"There's this bigger kid at her school, who keeps calling her Teensy-Weensy Whitney, because she's really, really small for her age, but you know, really cute, and so now all these other kids have started calling her that or just Weensy, and she said it's humiliating. I just can't understand why someone would be so mean to another kid at school!"

A voice at the other end of the table muttered, "Why not? You are."

Zoey's head popped up from working on her flowers. Who had said that? She looked down the table, and her eyes landed on the flushed cheeks of a sixth-grade girl named Lila, whom Zoey didn't know very well. She was shy and sweet and didn't speak up much. She was just the sort of person Ivy had probably picked on at some point.

Ivy, whose face had also turned scarlet, was staring around the table, looking for the culprit and appearing hurt. "I don't know who just said that, but it's not true. I mean, I know I'm not the nicest person in the world, but I'm not a *bully*. I mean, my poor cousin! The kid that's harassing her is an *actual* bully. I don't want you guys to think of me like that. I'm not like that. I'm not."

Ivy seemed to be arguing with herself. No one at the table spoke up, not even Sean. Zoey felt like, for the first time, Ivy might be realizing that whenever she said mean things, there was a *person* at the receiving end of those comments, and they got hurt. Maybe Ivy was even remembering the awful things she'd posted on Zoey's blog a while back, which had caused Zoey so much heartache.

"Oh my gosh, guys," Ivy said to the silent room. "Tell me if I'm ever like that again! Okay? *Please*."

"We will," Sean promised.

"You're not like that," Emily said finally. In Zoey's opinion, Emily could be a bit of a bully sometimes herself. "You're just popular, so people are jealous."

Ivy exhaled deeply. "Well, okay."

Zoey's phone buzzed. Even though she was fascinated by the epiphany Ivy seemed to be having, she couldn't resist checking her phone.

There was a new e-mail from Sonya Turley's costumer with photos of the finished costume! Zoey hurriedly clicked on the first thumbnail to see it enlarged. Unfortunately, she still couldn't see it well enough to really inspect it on her phone's small screen, but from what she could tell, it looked great. She clicked on the photo of the back of the outfit and was pleased by how beautiful the piano-key skirt looked. The belt detailing with the sequins was terrific, and she couldn't wait to see it on Sonya Turley for real.

"Zoey, what's going on over there?" Sean asked. "You're wearing the biggest smile I've ever seen!"

Everyone who had been sewing stopped and looked at Zoey expectantly.

Zoey blushed and put down her phone. She'd told her girlfriends about designing the ice-skater's costume, and she'd written about it on her blog, but she'd never told the fashion club. She didn't want them to think she was bragging or trying to seem better than they were. But since the costume was done, she couldn't help sharing her excitement.

"Well, guys, I designed an ice-skating costume, and Sonya Turley decided she wanted to wear it to nationals this weekend, and her costumer has just finished sewing it! She sent me a picture. And I'll get to see Sonya on TV actually wearing it when she skates for gold in the competition this weekend!"

The words tumbled out of Zoey, one on top of the other. She hadn't realized how excited she was about seeing her work on live TV until just that moment.

"I was wondering when you were going to mention that!" Sean said. "I read it on your blog weeks ago, but then you never told me in person."

"Wow!" said Lila. "That is the most amazingly coolest thing ever, Zoey!"

Zoey could feel herself still blushing. No matter how many good things happened with her design work, compliments were still embarrassing. She looked nervously at Ivy, waiting for the snarky comment that was sure to come. Probably something like, *Sonya Turley chose YOUR design? Is she color blind or something?*

But Ivy said no such thing. Instead, she smiled nicely, and said, "My grandmother and my cousin and I love watching ice-skating. We'll watch the competition at the nursing home together Saturday night and root for Sonya."

Zoey nodded, too stunned to reply. It hadn't exactly been praise for Zoey's accomplishment, but it had been nice. And that was something.

"Let's all watch the competition and root for Sonya—and Zoey. FFC is a team!" Sean declared. He held up his wrist with one of the FFC bracelets

Daphne Shaw had sent, and the rest of the group, including Ivy, did the same. Zoey looked down at her own wrist and noticed she'd forgotten to put hers on.

"Where's your bracelet, Zoey?" asked Emily, judgment in her voice.

"Shoot, I must have left it in my gym locker," Zoey lied. She didn't normally lie, but the disappointed faces looking back at her expected a good explanation. "I forgot to put it back on after volleyball."

Sean smiled at her, accepting her story easily. Zoey squirmed in her seat, unhappy that she'd felt like she had to lie, and unhappy also, that she remembered seeing the bracelet on her dresser that morning and hadn't even thought to put it on.

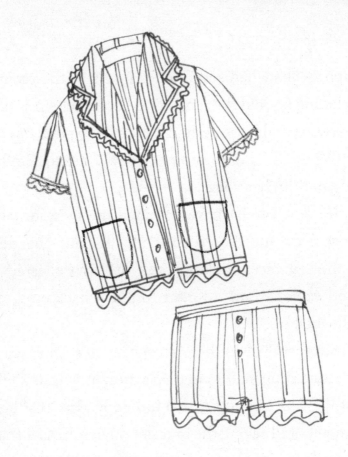

CHAPTER 12

The Perfect PJ's!

S challenged everyone in the Fashion Fun Club to try and use up all the free fabric we got from A Stitch in Time, so I've designed these pajamas from a blue and pink-striped flannel. I don't know about you, but I think flannel pj's usually get too hot at night! That's why

I chose to make this pair with short sleeves and shorts. And I had to add pockets because I love pockets, and the scalloped trim is to make them a little quirky . . . No one expects scalloped flannel pj's! Just looking at them makes me want to hit the snooze button. . . .☺

Readers, sometimes I feel like I spend half of my life sewing and the other half being *nervous* about what I've sewn. The ice-skating costume I designed for Sonya Turley will be making its TV debut tonight at the national championships! (In this case, I didn't do the actual *sewing*, but you know what I mean.) I don't think I've ever been this anxious about seeing one of my creations in action, except for maybe my aunt's wedding dress, and we all know how *that* turned out. Sheesh! (Okay, if you don't know, I forgot to stitch up one of the basted seams, so it came open while Lulu was dancing, and then I stepped on the hem of the dress and ripped the bottom, and long story short—the floor-length dress ended up being a knee-length dress for the second half of the reception!) I guess you could say it was a good learning experience!

Puh-lease watch the competition tonight and root for Sonya! And for my costume! And you can wear *your* favorite pj's while you watch!

Zoey's father decided that having something designed by his daughter appear on television warranted a viewing party, so he invited all of Zoey's friends, Aunt Lulu and Uncle John, and Allie over to watch.

Since the competition didn't start until seven o'clock, the group started the evening with chips, guacamole, and pizza. Everyone talked excitedly about seeing Zoey's outfit, except Zoey, whose stomach was tied up in knots. She was too nervous to even eat the pizza. She wondered if that's how Sonya felt every time she took to the ice! Sonya actually had to *perform* that evening, perfectly, and on ice! And all Zoey had to do was sit at home and watch.

When it was time for the show to begin, Zoey and her girlfriends headed into the living room. Mr. Webber, Lulu, John, Marcus, and Allie stayed in the kitchen to chat and instructed Zoey to call them in when Sonya came on. The nationals competition could be long, and the only people who really wanted to watch all the skaters were the girls.

Zoey and her friends plunked down on the sofa together, and lined their feet up on the coffee table in front of them.

"What's with Marcus and Allie?" Libby whispered. The TV was loud enough to drown out their conversation, but she still didn't want to risk being overheard.

"Yeah," said Priti. "They definitely weren't smiling during dinner, and Allie was sort of cranky."

Zoey shook her head. She'd noticed things between her brother and Allie had been different lately, too. But as Marcus's younger sister, and Allie's friend, her loyalty was torn. She wanted to stay out of their relationship completely, and the only way she could think to do that was to not ask either of them any questions about it, or to even let herself wonder what was going on.

"I don't know," Zoey said slowly. "But Marcus sighs a lot when she texts him."

"Young love," Priti joked. "It's never easy. And speaking of young love . . ." She turned to look at Kate.

Kate's cheeks immediately went red, but there

wasn't time for Priti to tease her because on the TV screen, Sonya Turley was taking the ice.

"Come in, everybody!" Priti yelled. "It's time!"

Everyone ran into the living room and shuffled around to get a good view of the TV. Zoey grabbed a throw pillow and squeezed it tightly to her chest. Her breath was stuck in her throat.

Then Sonya appeared in her peacock-blue costume. There was a gasp in the room. Even Zoey couldn't help gasping a little bit. It was so amazing to see her creation live!

"It looks wonderful!" Kate said, rubbing Zoey's back. "What a neat skirt."

Zoey had to admit the skirt flowed beautifully as Sonya skated to the center of the rink, just as she'd imagined it in her head. As *Rhapsody in Blue* began to play, Sonya launched into her routine, attacking her jumps and spins with energy and grace.

"She's wonderful!" Aunt Lulu said. "And your costume captures the music perfectly, Zoey. Bravo!"

Zoey began to relax slightly. The costume did look amazing. And Sonya was killing it.

The commentator, Clive Anzell, a former men's

figure-skating champion famous for wearing avant-garde fashions, said, "What a lovely and unique costume for a lovely and unique skater."

Zoey smiled and felt her cheeks heat up as everyone in the living room cheered for her.

Sonya cruised across the ice, preparing for the most difficult of all the triple jumps, the triple axel. Zoey's living room fell silent, and Sonya took off for her three-and-a-half rotations. She landed the jump, and the crowd exploded into applause, but a second later, Zoey's living room was still silent. No one was cheering.

The bottom hem of the beautiful car wash skirt had somehow gotten snagged on the sequin belt detail of Sonya's costume and tucked under itself.

"What happened back there?" asked Marcus. "It looks like she tucked the skirt into her underwear or something!"

"Quiet, Marcus," Allie snapped.

Mortified, Zoey covered her face with her hands. Her friends all immediately put their hands on her—her arms, her back, wherever—for support. They held their breath as Sonya continued her routine.

Zoey separated her fingers just enough to peek through them. Sonya was still skating her heart out, either unaware of what the back of her costume looked like or simply carrying on the way she was expected to. And while her skating was lovely, her wardrobe malfunction was distracting.

The silence continued for two painful minutes. To Zoey, they felt like eons.

"It's not like her underwear is *showing* or anything," Marcus said finally. "Or her butt. It's just that the skirt is all bunched up. It's not *that* big of a deal."

"Marcus, stop!" Allie hissed. "You're making it worse."

Zoey wasn't angry at her brother. She knew he was honestly trying to be helpful. But what he didn't understand was that the primary purpose of a skating costume is to look beautiful and *perform* during a skating routine. It wasn't supposed to have snags that made the entire country focus on Sonya Turley's behind for four whole minutes!

Clive, who had been gallantly trying to keep the conversation on her skating, finally said, "It looks

like Sonya might want to have a chat with her costumer after this performance. If she's going to be
landing triple axels in competition, she needs an
outfit that can handle it!"

The other commentator, a coach, replied, "These
costumes are usually vigorously tested through
many dress rehearsals. But I've never seen Sonya
wearing this one before. Maybe it's new, and they
didn't have time to take it for a test drive."

"She won't make *that* mistake again," Clive said.

Sonya's routine ended, and she curtsied to the
crowd. She skated around to pick up several of the
flowers and stuffed animals fans had thrown onto
the ice, waving to the crowd and smiling.

The camera then showed her coach, urgently
gesturing to her to adjust her skirt. At first Sonya
looked confused, then turned her head to look down
her back and saw the problem. She gamely swatted
at the skirt with her hand to get it to unsnag from
the sequins, smiled with a slight shrug, and skated
off the ice, as if she couldn't have cared less.

"Wow," breathed Kate. "She's amazing! She's so
poised."

"It's not like it's *that* big of a deal," Priti said. "Skirts move around. That's what they do. That's why I always wearing leggings or bike shorts underneath."

"But this is an *ice-skating* skirt," Zoey moaned. "It's not supposed to look like it's tucked into her underpants!"

Sonya sat down in the kiss 'n' cry booth to await her score. One of the reporters at the event ran over to ask her questions.

"Sonya, did you know your skirt was messed up like that? Did it make it hard for you to concentrate?"

Sonya smiled serenely, even though she was still waiting for her score. "I didn't know. All I cared about was landing my triple axel, which I did!"

Mr. Webber clapped. "That's right, Sonya! Remind the audience what really matters."

Sonya's score finally appeared, and it was a personal best for her long program! She stood up and took a bow, flipping her skirt with her hand, as if to poke fun at the situation.

"Turn it off now, please," Zoey pleaded. "And someone bring me a slice of pizza!"

Aunt Lulu ran to the kitchen to get her a slice.

"You know," said Libby gently, "it was your design, but you didn't *sew* the costume. The costumer is a professional and should have been able to fix that. Or they should have done a dress rehearsal, like the commentator said."

"I know," said Zoey. "But I can't help feeling responsible because I'm the designer! She never would have been wearing that costume if it weren't for me."

"Stop beating yourself up, Zoey!" Priti ordered. "I mean it!"

With a sympathetic smile, Lulu placed a slice of pizza in front of Zoey. She ushered the family and Allie back to the kitchen, leaving Zoey alone with her girlfriends. Lulu seemed to understand that sometimes a girl just needed to be alone and wallow with her pals.

Kate, who must have been desperate to change the subject, blurted out, "So I had another date with Tyler last night."

Priti leaped on her. "You did? TELL!"

Kate looked at Zoey, to make sure it was okay

that she had started talking about something else. Zoey nodded gratefully.

"Well, it was kind of weird, actually. We went to a movie, then out for ice cream afterward, and it seemed like he kept saying what I wanted to hear instead of whatever he really thought."

"What do you mean?" asked Libby.

"Like he kept talking about how he liked soccer because it's a 'low-scoring game,' and that makes each goal so much more thrilling, which is exactly what I think. But he's never even *played* soccer and doesn't seem to watch it on TV, from what I can tell. And then when we got ice cream, he went ahead and ordered us both hot fudge sundaes, without asking me first! It was like he already knew my favorite thing without even asking."

"I don't think any of that is weird," Priti insisted. "Soccer *is* a low-scoring game, and tons of people like hot fudge sundaes. Maybe you're just a perfect match!"

Kate frowned. "But it feels . . . off. Like he knows me already, but he doesn't. You know?"

Zoey couldn't take it anymore. Maybe she was

just too upset about Sonya's costume, or maybe she was tired of Kate being so determined not to like a nice boy simply because he wasn't very athletic and seemed able to guess what she liked without having to ask first.

"Oh, for crying out loud, Kate, it was me!" said Zoey. "I've been helping Tyler."

The shock on Kate's face was awful to see. Zoey felt like Kate was looking at her as if she didn't know her at all.

"You've been *what?*" Kate said.

Zoey nodded her head. "He e-mailed me before your first date and told me he liked you a lot. He asked me what a few of your favorite things were. It was *very innocent*, I promise. And really sweet. And then he's e-mailed me a few other times to ask me things like your favorite ice cream, flower, color, whatever. It wasn't really *personal* stuff, I swear!"

Kate's eyes grew dark. "So that's how he knew to bring me a daisy. Because you told him I loved daisies! Zoey, how could you? How can I find out if I actually have anything in common with him, or trust how I feel about him, when you're telling him what to do and say? I want him to be himself! Otherwise, what's the point?"

"Listen, Kate," Zoey snapped. "If it weren't for *us*, you wouldn't have even given that boy a chance. You were so close-minded about him not playing sports! He's a nice guy!"

"That's for *me* to decide, not you! And in my opinion, someone who e-mails my best friend behind my back to spy on me doesn't seem so nice! It seems sneaky!"

Zoey looked to Priti and Libby for backup. She knew they thought Kate was being awfully tough on Tyler too.

But Priti stayed uncharacteristically silent, and Libby sat looking down at her hands. Neither of them were used to hearing Kate and Zoey argue.

"You don't understand," Kate went on. "I'm under enough pressure! My parents are so excited a boy has been calling me, and I'm *finally* interested in something other than soccer or swimming, they're practically planning my wedding! They keep telling me to invite him over for dinner, and they want to make plans to meet his *parents*. Seriously!"

Priti looked sympathetic. "That's a little crazy."

Kate nodded. "Exactly. I'm just not ready for all of this. I was hoping to get to know him slowly and *see* if I liked him enough for it to be worth all this bother. But between you and my parents, it's too much!"

Zoey didn't know what to say. She had no idea Kate's parents were so into the idea of Kate dating, but she did know they were always trying to get her to join clubs at school she had no interest in, just to keep her from being a total tomboy.

The doorbell rang, and Libby hopped up to get it. It was Mrs. Holbrooke, ready to take Priti and Libby home.

Since Kate just lived a few houses up the street, she normally would just walk. But with a swift look at Zoey, Kate said, "Mrs. Holbrooke, would you mind dropping me at my house too? I don't feel like walking tonight, and I'm ready to leave now."

Mrs. Holbrooke looked at Zoey questioningly, as if she could sense the tension in the room. But Zoey kept her face blank.

"Of course, Kate," Mrs. Holbrooke said. "I'd be happy to."

Priti and Libby said good-bye to Zoey and yelled thank-you to Mr. Webber in the kitchen. Kate stayed quiet, pretending to be very busy putting on her jacket. Then the girls left, without Zoey and Kate saying a single word to each other.

Zoey couldn't remember a time when she or Kate had walked away mad at each other. Not one single time.

How could a few innocent e-mails have gone so terribly wrong?

------------ CHAPTER 13 ------------

Zipping it!

I think I may have really messed up, readers.☺ I usually think of myself as a pretty open person, ready to try new things, meet new people, and like everyone! But lately I think I've been a little close-minded. There's a person I know who I've always sort of written off as just a meanie and not bothered trying to be nice to her. But recently this person seems to have matured a bit, or lightened up, or something. And I'm the only one who hasn't been willing to give her another chance! (Probably because I've been burned by her too many times to count.) But I think it's probably time that I do.

Even *worse*, I think I've been close-minded toward one of my own besties, because I interfered (kindly! I meant it kindly!) in her love life, which I should *never* have done. And all because I assumed I knew what was best for her better than she did. Why didn't I remind myself what a smart girl she is and how she always, always makes good decisions? Why did I think I was so right about everything? Sigh. I think I'm ready to finally stop being *close-minded*, and get back to just being *clothes-minded*! (Ha! Did you see that coming?)

What do you think of this fantastic white faux-leather jacket? Wouldn't you love to wear it while sitting on the bleachers, watching a soccer game, like I will be this weekend, rooting for my oldest and dearest pal, if she'll please forgive me? I should have kept my mouth shut instead of telling a certain someone what she liked and disliked. Notice all the zippers? I officially promise to "zip it" from now on and not be anyone's Cyrano de Bergerac. I'm *sew* sorry, K. . . .

It was Monday morning yet again. In her usual sleepy, Monday fog, Zoey ate breakfast, packed her backpack, and rode the bus, sitting next to Kate as usual. Kate's hair was in its customary messy ponytail, and she was wearing cuffed jeans and an old faded camp T-shirt. A typical Kate outfit. But other than that, nothing was the same. Kate barely said a word to Zoey the whole ride, so Zoey tried to give her some space.

Before lunch, Zoey trudged to her locker, thinking about the response paper she needed to write for English class and what it was she was supposed to remember to bring in for science the next day. A rock? Some aluminum foil? She had no idea.

When she turned the corner of the hallway where her locker was, she stopped short. Kate was there, waiting there for her.

Kate stood leaning against the lockers. Zoey had never been so happy to see someone. Kate was holding note cards in her hand and studying them, unaware Zoey had arrived.

"Hey, there," Zoey said to catch her attention. "What are you studying for?"

"The Spanish quiz," Kate replied. Her grip on the cards tightened visibly as she looked up at Zoey. "I read your blog apology. Your, um, blog-pology."

"Apolobloggy? Abloggogy?" Zoey joked, glad to relieve some of the tension.

Kate half smiled. "You weren't the only one being close-minded, by the way. I was too, toward Tyler. It's just that from the moment I mentioned him to you guys and my parents, everyone's been pushing us to be boyfriend and girlfriend! And I didn't know anything about him yet. I still don't, really."

"I'm so, so sorry, Kate. You're totally right! How can you decide if you like someone when he's just doing things to please you? But I totally get it now—even *friendly* intervention in someone's love life is not okay. I will *never* be your Cyrano again!"

"*Good*," said Kate. Then she added, "I'd still like you to be my fashion consultant, though, for the rare occasions when I really care about what I'm wearing. But it won't be for dates any time soon! I thought a lot yesterday, and I called Tyler and told him I just wasn't ready to date yet. Like, anyone. I just want to be friends with him. And he was cool about it."

"Wait, what?" said Priti as she appeared beside them. "I hate to interrupt you guys making up, but, Kate, did you seriously tell Tyler you won't go out with him again?"

Kate sighed heavily. "*Yes.* And I don't want to talk about it anymore, Priti!"

Priti bit her lip and smiled. "Well, that's unfortunate. Because I'd just come up with the perfect couple name for you guys—Kyler! Or maybe Tylate. No, Kateler."

Kate laughed and punched Priti on the shoulder. "No, thank you. I'm back to being myself—just a regular girl who loves soccer, volunteering, and hanging with her friends. It's such a relief!"

"And I'm back to just being a designer instead of a ventriloquist," Zoey said jokingly. "Did I tell you Sonya Turley sent me an e-mail about the ice-skating costume?" She fished her phone from her bag, located the e-mail, and read it aloud. "'Thanks for the design, Zoey! It was really beautiful, and my backside now has its own Twitter account. My coach says any publicity is good publicity, and hey, at least I won the silver medal!'"

"She has a sense of humor," said Priti. "I like that. She's about, what, fifteen years old? Maybe *she'd* be good with Tyler?"

Kate smiled. "Nah—wouldn't work. She's too athletic."

"But remember? Opposites attract," pushed Priti. "Well, sometimes. And only if they want to."

The girls laughed and looped their arms together as they headed to lunch. Zoey had her best girlfriend back. Whatever she'd forgotten for Science class (was it plastic bags?) didn't matter much at all.

By the end of the day on Tuesday, it hit Zoey that it was her turn again to come up with an activity for the fashion club. She'd been so busy with schoolwork, volunteering, and studying that she hadn't had a second to think of anything. She looked through the ideas in the comments section of her Sew Zoey post asking for club ideas, but everything sounded too complicated. She remembered mentioning to a few of the club members that she'd been teaching herself to knit and wondered if she could ask Mrs. Holmes if the school had some knitting needles everyone could use to learn a few basic stitches. She only had one set at home. She told Sean the idea in home ec, and he quickly approved it.

But when the end of the day Wednesday came, Zoey had forgotten to ask Mrs. Holmes and found herself rushing, yet again, just to be five minutes late to the meeting. When she arrived, Sean was there, having already set up the room by himself and borrowed the knitting needles from Mrs. Holmes. They were passed out to club members, along with skeins of yarn, and everyone was staring at Zoey expectantly, ready to begin.

Zoey apologized profusely and got right down to business, teaching everyone how to cast on, and to knit one, purl one (the seed stitch!).

The group began trying to make their own stitches. Josie mentioned she'd had some experience knitting before, but she was having trouble getting her purl stitches to stay smooth.

Ivy leaned over and looked at Josie's work, saying, "It doesn't look like you've *that* done much knitting before. Yours looks the same as mine!" Ivy proudly held up her bumpy bit of knitting to show the group.

"*Ivy,*" Zoey chastised reflexively. "Cut it out."

"C'mon, Zoey—I didn't mean it like that at *all*. I was just teasing her. You know, like normal friends tease one another."

Zoey had never heard Ivy refer to Josie as a friend, but Josie smiled back at Ivy and didn't seem bothered by the comment in the slightest. So Zoey was forced to accept that maybe Ivy really was trying to be nicer, and she just needed some practice to be as nice as a regular person.

Be open-minded, Zoey told herself. And she repeated it several times.

As the group began working independently on their knitting, Sean gestured to Zoey to come and talk to him in the corner, opposite from where Mrs. Holmes sat doing some grading.

Zoey went reluctantly, because she knew what a terrible, unprepared treasurer and VP she was. She never wore her FFC bracelet or scarf, she'd still only collected dues from half the group, and she was never on time to meetings. The truth was, she dreaded fashion club each week, and not because of Ivy. While she'd like the idea of the club in theory, in reality, it took away from her own sketching and sewing time. It was a lot of responsibility that she didn't feel she wanted to balance with her Sew Zoey blog and business, and, in all honesty, it was so much more fun to go to the pet shelter and volunteer when she had free time! Puppies and kittens were just better, and nice for a change of pace.

But she had made a promise to Sean to help him with the club, and now she was stuck. Zoey did not want to be someone who broke her promises. It was a Webber family rule.

"I'm sorry I was late," Zoey said quickly, before Sean could even speak. "And I didn't mean to snap at Ivy just now. I'm still getting used to the new her."

Sean's eyes crinkled as he smiled, putting his

hands on her shoulders. "I don't know how to tell you this, Zoey, but you're fired."

She couldn't believe what she'd just heard. "*Fired?*"

He nodded, still smiling. "It's a mercy firing. You don't want to be here, and you really are a terrible treasurer. So I'm letting you off the hook. You can still be our, um, Fashion Fun Club *consultant*, if you want, and come by sometimes. But I can handle this, and you're too busy with all your Sew Zoey stuff, anyway."

"Thank you, Sean," Zoey said gratefully. "You just might be my favorite new friend."

He looked guilty for a second. "You won't think that when I tell you who I plan to nominate as your replacement."

"Who?"

He leaned close and whispered. "*Ivy.*"

Zoey laughed, and the group looked over at them from their knitting. Zoey made her face serious once again and whispered to Sean, "Well, she did pay her dues. And she does show up on time. So she's got me beat there, already."

"And she's awfully good at knitting," Sean said. "Ha-ha."

Sean and Zoey returned to the group, and Zoey spent the rest of the meeting—her *last* fashion club meeting—helping everyone master the basics of knitting. She felt good when their session was over. She'd tried the club, and it hadn't worked out. Because sometimes things just don't, like with Kate and Tyler. But it was still worth trying.

As Zoey was packing up to leave, Ivy said, "Josie, did you watch the ice-skating championship this past weekend?"

"*Non!* Some of my cousins were visiting from France and I missed it. *Dis-moi,* what happened?"

Zoey braced herself for Ivy's response. The only thing worse than watching Sonya's wardrobe malfunction live would be to listen to Ivy describe it in detail to a roomful of people.

"Oh, it was great," Ivy said, to Zoey's surprise. "Sonya Turley got the silver! And her costume was beautiful. A really inventive car wash-style skirt."

Zoey looked over at Ivy, to see if she was holding back laughter, or if she really was planning to skip the part where Zoey's design had gone terribly wrong.

But Ivy's face was calm and happy as she continued to knit, and she didn't even appear to notice Zoey looking at her. Ivy was just complimenting Zoey's work, seemingly with no agenda.

Maybe the Fashion Fun Club had changed Ivy for the better. Or maybe her cousin being bullied, or spending time volunteering at the home for the elderly, had made a difference. Whatever it was, Zoey wondered if it would last. Was the meanest mean girl of Mapleton Prep really becoming a nice girl?

Zoey hoped so. Either way, she couldn't wait to start some new Sew Zoey projects, now that she'd been officially fired from the fashion club and would have more free time. New projects were always fun . . . and all she needed to do to find her next one was to stay *clothes*-minded, and open-minded, too!

Be *clothes* minded, not close-minded. . . .
Turn the page for a sneak peek at the next book in the Sew Zoey series:

DRESSED
TO
FRILL

Fired Up

I know you're not supposed to enjoy being "fired" from a job, but I've been all "fired up" with new ideas for outfits since getting kicked out as treasurer of the Fashion Fun Club. Aunt Lulu said maybe the club was too much of a good thing. That sometimes you need to take a break and do something completely different (and for me, that means *not* sewing related), so your mind can wander to new and exciting creative places. It's also really nice to have time to do nothing at all!

That's why I love volunteering at the pet shelter. With all those adorable dogs and cats to walk and play with, you never know what's going to happen next. I always come away with more energy for my sewing projects.

We're starting the next elective in school soon. I'm excited to try industrial arts. I wonder if I can somehow figure out how to combine woodworking and fashion. But how would you sit down in a wooden dress? Hmm . . . will clearly have to give this a bit more thought. ☺

"I need your advice," Kate Mackey announced to her best friends, Zoey Webber, Priti Holbrooke, and Libby Flynn. "I'm thinking of giving Tyler another chance."

The girls were in their pajamas, lounging around on Libby's bed. It was sleepover night at the Flynn house.

"What made you decide that?" Zoey asked. Kate had broken up with Tyler Landon, who'd had a crush on her, a few weeks earlier after only a few dates, partially due to Zoey's misguided attempts to help him woo her. Under Zoey's helpful advice (which turned out to be not so helpful after all!), Tyler had been behaving differently than usual because he'd thought it would make Kate like him.

"Well . . . we have a great time together when we volunteer at the food pantry," Kate said.

"Not to mention the fact that he's *super*cute," Priti observed.

Kate blushed. "Well, yes, there *is* that," she admitted. "But also he's promised just to be himself this time."

Now it was Zoey's turn to blush.

"I was only trying to help," she said for what must have been the umpteenth time since her matchmaking fiasco.

"I know," Kate said, smiling. "All is forgiven . . . Really."

"Whew!" Zoey exhaled, relieved. "I'd hate to think I completely ruined everything."

"You guys seem to have a lot of fun when we're at the food pantry," Libby observed. She'd started volunteering there, in addition to her school community service at the pet shelter, so she had seen Kate and Tyler together.

"I'm glad you've decided to give Tyler another chance," Zoey told Kate. "What if I'd messed up the course of true love?"

"*True love?!*" Kate exclaimed. "Let's not go overboard. I just think he's nice. And funny."

"And supercute," Priti added.

"I guess," Kate mumbled, blushing a little.

"Well, now that we've agreed that Tyler is supercute, can I show you something superexciting?" Libby asked.

"Yes, please!" Priti said.

Libby jumped off the bed and went to her desk.

"Look! Hot off the press!" she said, holding out an embossed card threaded with gold ribbon. "My Bat Mitzvah invitation. Isn't it cool?"

"It's beautiful!" Priti exclaimed.

"I love the gold ribbon," Zoey said. "It makes the lettering pop."

"And the gold lining inside the envelope matches the lettering and the ribbon," Kate observed. "So pretty!"

Libby climbed back onto the bed and sat crossed-legged.

"A few years ago, I wasn't even sure I was going to have a Bat Mitzvah. Dad's Catholic and Mom's Jewish, but neither of them are that religious. We celebrate all the holidays, but more the traditions than the religious stuff," she explained.

"So what made you change your mind?" Zoey asked.

"My grandpa," Libby said. "He only just escaped the Holocaust as a young boy. In fact, his name wasn't Van Langen when he was born. But his parents hid him with non-Jewish neighbors when my great-grandparents were sent to a concentration camp. And then . . . Well, they didn't come back after the war, and he ended up adopting the name of the family who hid him and saved his life."

"That's so sad," Kate said. "He never saw his parents again?"

"Never," Libby said, shaking her head. "And he hardly ever talked about it until recently, when he said it would mean a lot to him if I had a Bat Mitzvah. So that's why I decided to do it. But it's *so much* work, which is the reason I haven't been around as much lately."

"I've never been to a Bat Mitzvah before," Zoey admitted. "What do you do? What do *we* do? And more to the point, what do we *wear*?"

The girls all laughed.

"Zoey always gets right down to the important questions," Priti said.

"Well, there'll be a service in the synagogue," Libby explained, then reached over to the bedside table and picked up some papers. "And I have to read a section of the Torah in Hebrew. I've been going to a tutor, and practicing my Torah portion every night before I go to bed, and listening to tapes so I get the pronunciation right. See?"

Zoey looked at the unfamiliar alphabet. "It looks like Greek to me."

"Ha!" Libby said. "It felt like Greek to me when I first started. Except now that I've been studying it for a while, I can tell it's Hebrew, even though it's still hard to read."

"I can't believe how much work you have to do," Priti said. "It's really great that you're doing this for your grandpa."

"It's not just for him. It's become important to me too," Libby said. "But I also have to make a speech, which I'm really nervous about. But on the plus side, I get to have a really fun party after the service."

"Party? Did you say party?" Priti perked up immediately.

"I've been to a Bar Mitzvah party before—it was really fun," Kate said. "They played lots of games, and the food was amazing."

"Yeah, Mom and I met with the caterers last week," Libby said. "The theme of my Bat Mitzvah is going to be 'Sweet,' so needless to say we're going to have yummy desserts!"

"So . . . you read from the scrolls during a service, and then there's a big party with yummy desserts? That's a Bat Mitzvah?" Zoey asked, wanting to make sure she had it straight.

"That's not all," Libby said. "I also do a mitzvah project, which means doing something to make the world a better place by helping others."

"What's your project?" Kate asked.

"Well, since I started volunteering at the food pantry, I've noticed they only give out canned and packaged goods, which must get really boring and isn't as healthy as having fresh produce," Libby said. "So I've started a vegetable patch to grow fresh produce to donate there. Dad helped me."

"But that sounds like even more hard work," Priti groaned. "Are you going to have time for any *fun*?"

Libby laughed. "Gardening *is* fun. Come over and help me weed sometime! Maybe next Sunday?"

Priti looked skeptical. "Hmm . . . sounds like a great time . . . ," she said. "But I think I'm busy that day. Or any day when getting dirt under my finger-nails is involved!"

"Do you get lots of presents?" Kate asked. "The kid whose Bar Mitzvah I went to did."

"Well, yes," Libby said.

"Who are you inviting?" Zoey asked.

"About a zillion relatives, half of whose names I don't even remember; kids from school—Josie, Gabe, Miles; Tyler since I got to know him at the food pantry; a bunch of my friends from Sunday school; and . . . Emily."

Great stories are like great accessories: You can never have too many! Collect all the books in the Sew Zoey series:

Ready to Wear

On Pins and Needles

Lights, Camera, Fashion!

Stitches and Stones

Cute as a Button

A Tangled Thread

Knot Too Shabby!

Swatch Out!

A Change of Lace

Bursting at the Seams

Clothes Minded

Dressed to Frill

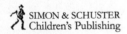

Like reading about Zoey's adventures? Double your fun with twins Alex and Ava in the It Takes Two series!